BEARLY TOGETHER

ZOE CHANT

GREEN VALLEY SHIFTERS

This is book four of the Green Valley Shifters series. All of my books are stand-alones (they never have cliffhangers!) and can be read independently, but this book does reference some of the events in the previous books and bring back some favorite characters. This is the order the series may be most enjoyed:

CHAPTER 1

Someone had handed Shelley a baby.

Shelley was too surprised to thrust it back before the golden-haired woman who gave it to her was hurrying off after another small shrieking person, and then she was stuck with it.

The squishy little thing stared at her with big blue eyes and made a bubble with its tiny alien mouth.

It was almost hairless, and it smelled weird.

Shelley tried to give it to the woman that her father had just married, but Tawny only laughed. "Patricia will be back in a few moments," the white-haired woman said cheerfully. "Look, she likes you." Then she hurried off to supervise something concerning food.

Shelley looked at the thing in her arms with horror as it squirmed and flailed chubby fists.

"You're my aunt, Shelley," a suspicious voice said from her waist, and Shelley looked down to find a little dark-haired boy staring up at her.

"You're my nephew, Trevor," Shelley agreed crossly. Was she supposed to be supporting the thing's head? It was a little uncomfortable where it was lying in the crook of her elbow staring at her; did she dare adjust it? What if she dropped it? She'd rather let her arms cramp up in place than risk it.

Trevor squinted up at her. "Are you Grandpa Powell's favorite?"

Shelley looked down at the boy in consternation. "Who would tell you that?"

"Oh, Trevor, no…" Shaun, her brother, looked mortified as he came into the sunny little room filled with plants where Shelly had been waylaid with the infant. "I swear I didn't mean him to hear that… kids, they absorb everything…" he sputtered.

Shelley tried to carefully extricate the baby from her arms. "Take this thing and I will pretend it never happened. Besides," she told Trevor, "*you* are now Grandpa Powell's favorite and you are welcome to it."

Trevor grinned at her. "I thought so. It's cuz…" The boy clapped a hand over his mouth as if he had been about to reveal state secrets. "I CAN'T TELL YOU!" he shouted, and to Shelley's relief, he fled the room.

One down, one to get rid of.

"We're trying not make a big deal out favorites and the whole… shifting thing…." Shaun said, in that disapproving, big brother *I know better* tone he'd always been perfect at.

"Sorry," Shelley said without apology. "I don't really… do kids. About the best you're going to get out of me is that I'll try not to swear around him or let him play with sharp things. Much. Will you please take this thing before I break it?"

To her relief, Shaun willingly put out his hands for the infant. "This is Victoria, Patricia's new daughter."

But Victoria had a drooly fistful of Shelley's hair and a grip on her shirt now, and she was bizarrely bendy and uncooperative for something so small and made out of butter. "Oh good God, she's thrown up on my Chanel," Shelley realized in horror as she tried to peel the minuscule fingers from the silk blouse without damaging the fabric. "Ow! How can something that small have a grip like that?!" The baby was tugging on her hair now, delighting in Shelley's grimaces of pain.

Shaun actually laughed, not offering to help.

The mother who'd left the baby with her in the first place returned to find Shelley trying to pry the infant off of her, pleading, "Get it off me! There is *vomit* on my blouse!"

She was embarrassed and frankly terrified; she didn't want to accidentally harm the uncooperative baby, and everyone was smirking and giggling at her rising panic.

"Here, I'll take her," Patricia said with a smile that Shelley was too humiliated to find kind. "Thank you for holding her."

The baby finally let go and went willingly to Patricia, bouncing easily in her arms and burbling happily.

"Sorry," Shelley said tightly, knowing she'd done a terrible job at a simple task. "I'm not a baby person." She wanted to sink into a hole and die.

She focused on the blouse, because outrage seemed better than a panic attack over the way that everyone was looking at her. "I need to soak this stain before the shirt is ruined," she said stiffly. "Excuse me."

She heard Shaun make excuses for her as she stalked out. "Sorry, that's my sister. She's got a thing about her clothes."

It's not clothes, she wanted to stop and protest, but what else would they assume? That she was afraid of kids?

3

CHAPTER 2

*D*ean looked up from his paperwork at the jingle of the store door and bit back a groan. Possibly the only thing worse than quarterly tax estimates had just walked in.

"Good morning, Gillian," he said with all the patience he could dredge up.

"Good morning, Dean!" she trilled in return. "Isn't it a beautiful morning?"

"Sure is," Dean said briefly. He hoped that bending back over his papers with his calculator would be enough to dissuade her, but he wasn't particularly surprised when she didn't take the hint, coming to lean on the counter conversationally.

"How's your darling little Aaron doing?" she pried.

"He's doing great," Dean said politely. "He likes first grade. How are your kids? And *Brad?*" Being married didn't seem to keep Gillian from being very obvious about her predatory ways. She was ten years older than Dean, at least, and not unattractive, but Dean was not the slightest bit interested and the woman would not take a hint.

4

"They're great," Gillian said airily. "Really busy at school. Brad's *away* a lot."

Dean nodded. "Mm-hmm." What kind of expense was a ream of paper? And if he took a roll of duct tape from inventory and used it to tape Gillian's mouth shut, how did he account for that? Did it become an office supply?

"I hear there's snow in the forecast for next week," she said, playing with the display of carpenter pencils on the counter.

"Early, but not unheard of," Dean sighed. "Can I help you with something?"

"I've got a slow drain in the kitchen," Gillian said, giving him a look from under her eyelashes. "I'm just not sure what *parts* I might need."

"Have you tried Draino?" Dean suggested.

"That stuff is so toxic," Gillian said. "I just hate to use it."

"Can you remove the trap and check for a clog there?"

"Oh, that sounds so complicated," Gillian said, managing to lean over so that her cleavage was trying to make a jiggly escape from her shirt. "I'm sure I couldn't do that *myself*. Oh, but *you're* good at that stuff," she said, as if it had just occurred to her. "Could you come by and take a look? I just know you could figure it out."

Dean wondered if he had the word 'sucker' tattooed on his forehead and ran his hand through his hair. He needed a haircut.

"I don't mind paying," Gillian said coaxingly. "I know things are tight for you and Aaron."

The jingle of the store door was the sweetest sound that Dean had ever heard. "Sorry," he said, hoping he sounded a little more sorry than he felt. "Have a lot to take care of here."

"Hey Dean," Turner called. "You got a five-eighth ratchet head? I don't need a whole set."

Dean showed him personally where the clearance bin of broken sets was. "Don't know if we've got that size, but there's a chance."

Gillian, pouting, purchased a half gallon of Draino and gave him a lingering gaze as she left.

"Find what you needed?" Dean asked Turner. "The common sizes usually get snapped up fast."

"Didn't need one," Turner said with a chuckle. "Came in for a snow shovel, but those are right up front. Figured I'd look like an idiot asking you to point those out to me."

Dean smiled gratefully at Turner. "Thanks, Chief." Turner was in charge of the three-man local fire department.

"She's shameless," Turner said, shaking his graying head. "And you're not great at saying no."

"Give me some credit," Dean protested. "I have standards!"

"She doesn't," Turner scoffed.

"Hold on, now…" Dean laughed. "I think I've been insulted."

Turner picked out a snow shovel and Dean rang him up.

The third jingle from the store door might have been a record number of customers in an hour, but this one was only Henry, shuffling in looking—if possible—more disheveled than ever.

"Got any work?" Henry asked. He always looked a bit like he expected someone to kick him.

Dean looked down at his taxes. "Yeah, could you just watch things for a little bit? I've got to get this postmarked today." It was just an estimate; he could probably call what he'd already figured up good enough.

Henry's eyes brightened. "Sure," he said, standing taller.

Dean swiftly wrote out a check for entirely too much money and found a twenty-year-old envelope to stuff it into. The seal tasted bad and didn't seem to want to stick, so he ended up closing the envelope with a strip of duct tape.

"I'll be back in a bit," he said.

Outside, Green Valley was in full autumn color.

Trees along the lanes sported gold and orange and red, and merry breezes sent swirling leaves along the sidewalks. People were out raking their lawns, or mowing them one last time before the overnight frosts sent them into their long brown hibernation.

The mention of hibernation made his bear make a sleepy murmur of longing. It had been a long time since Dean had taken an opportunity to get out and stretch on four paws. He was overdue for slipping out into the woods around Green Valley for a little time in his other form.

Dean mailed his letter at the little post office and gathered the business mail from his box. Bills. Lots of bills.

He looked through them wistfully. He wasn't sure how his life had gotten where it was, and he couldn't imagine it any differently, but he couldn't help thinking that something was missing.

CHAPTER 3

*J*n a fresh shirt, with her hair brushed and her make-up touched up, Shelley felt considerably better.

"I know you were planning to head out tomorrow, but you are welcome to stay a few days," Tawny told her when she ventured back down to the kitchen. "The house came with several spare bedrooms, and if I have guests in them, I can't accidentally fill them up with books."

Shelley laughed because it was expected of her. Everyone else was thankfully gone; evening was falling, and probably they were all putting their sticky children into bed.

"Thank you, Tawny," she said genuinely; she did honestly like the woman her dad had just married. "I plan to leave tomorrow, but I was hoping to have someone look at my car before I left. It's making a terrible rattling noise every time I go over bumps and I don't want to get stranded halfway back to Minneapolis. Is there a good shop in town?"

Tawny handed her a piece of carrot from the cutting

board she was working on before Shelley could tell her that she didn't like carrots.

She put it down at the edge of the cutting board when Tawny turned back to the sink to wash her hands.

"There's only one shop in town," Tawny said cheerfully. "And it's great. Dean owns Ted's Hardware, and his shop is right next door. You can't miss it."

As advertised, it was impossible to miss the auto shop next to the hardware store. The town wasn't big enough that you could miss anything even if you wanted to.

Shelley pulled up in front of the single garage door and walked carefully around to the side door with its crooked 'OPEN' sign in the window. The sidewalk was cracked, and the last thing she needed to do was snap off a heel.

Open seemed to be a slight exaggeration.

There was a tall, greasy-looking counter in the tiny room with an old-fashioned register as well as a modern credit card machine (to Shelley's relief). There was a pile of take-out menus that also gave her a moment of hope... until she noticed that they were all from Madison. It was too much to believe that there could be decent food in Green Valley to eat while they did the diagnosis of her car.

Two chairs with cracked vinyl seats flanked a water dispenser with a leaning stack of tiny paper cups. The entertainment selection—and for that matter the decor— seemed to be limited to car magazines and farm economic journals. An open door behind the counter led out to the shop, to one side was a closed door that said 'Ted's Hardware,' and a smaller door open in the corner suggested a restroom that no amount of money in the world could have convinced Shelley to use.

"Hello?" she called hesitantly.

"Yeah?"

The man who suddenly sat up from behind the counter

had clearly been sleeping. Shelley had a moment of wondering if a homeless man had wandered in.

"I… have a problem with my car," Shelley said cautiously, looking around. She was beginning to think it was worth the risk just to drive to the city.

"I'm Henry; I'll check you in. Dean'll be back in a few. He had to walk to the post office."

A pad of carbon copy paper was put on the counter and a drawer was rummaged for a pen. "Make and model?"

"Lincoln Continental," Shelley said.

The scruffy man whistled. "Nice. We don't get so many of those, you know. Lotta tractors. Subarus. Pickups."

She gave him the rest of her details and very reluctantly passed him her key. "Is there a Starbucks nearby?" she asked plaintively. "Or some place with coffee? Maybe WiFi?" She knew there was decent coffee at her brother Shaun's bakery, but this was the one day a week he was closed.

"Best coffee in town is Gran's Grits," Henry said helpfully. "Two blocks over past the Presbyterian church across from the liquor store. I dunno about WiFi, but there's a television in the kitchen."

"Thank you," Shelley said primly. "Do you know how long it will take?"

"Oh, I dunno. Maybe an hour?" Henry guessed. "Course, if we gotta order parts, it might be longer."

Shelley could imagine no torture worse than being trapped in Green Valley several extra days. Maybe her insurance would cover a rental. It was probably worth paying for a rental out of pocket if the alternative was being stuck here.

"I'll be back in an hour," she said firmly.

"You do that," Henry said cheerfully.

CHAPTER 4

*D*ean furrowed his brow at the unexpected car in his garage. A Lincoln Continental was not the type of vehicle that any locals drove.

Well, not any of the *real* locals. There had been an influx of big city billionaires over the past few years; first Lee Montgomery who owned a bunch of big construction companies came in and married his daughter's preschool teacher. Then there had been Shaun Powell, some kind of financial investor, who'd followed the trend by marrying *his* son's preschool teacher. And just this summer, Shaun's big shot engineer father, Damien, had surprised the whole town by sweeping spinster Tawny Summers off her feet.

This wasn't a car any of those men drove, which meant someone new, and Dean sourly wondered if there were any other preschool teachers in town to romance.

Then he had a moment of hope; maybe they would run off with Gillian, and save the whole town a lot of trouble.

"Got a car to look at," Henry told him helpfully as he

came into the office, waving a ticket at him. "Some fancy lady with clicky shoes and red lips."

Dean was disappointed for a moment, then hoped briefly that maybe Gillian's man-eating ways really hid a closeted interest in women. *That* would certainly keep the town talking for a while. He squinted at the paper Henry gave him. "What's the problem, exactly?" he asked. Henry's handwriting was awful, and the problem probably wasn't a rattlesnake.

"Rattles going over bumps, she said," he explained. "Worried about getting back to the city if it was something major."

Dean looked at the name on the key fob. Shelley Powell. She must be related to Shaun and Damien, he thought.

"I'll take a look," Dean said. "Thanks for watching the counter." He gave the man a certificate to Gran's Grits. Cash in Henry's hands would be spent at all the wrong places, but he didn't want the man to starve, so he gave him what work he could do (and remembered to show up for) and paid under the counter in gift certificates to local stores.

Henry took the certificate with a grin. "Much appreciated," he said sincerely, giving a courtly bow. "I'll be back tomorrow."

He probably wouldn't be.

He sauntered out as if Dean had just given him a golden ticket, whistling his way off-key down the street.

Dean turned on the shop radio and put the bell back up on the counter; Henry had put it on the floor for some reason.

Ten minutes and a test drive later, it sang out demandingly and Dean pushed himself out from beneath the car with a disparaging snort.

Rich city people, he thought derisively. This one probably couldn't even pump her own gas.

He was wiping his hand off with a rag, trying to come up with a diplomatic way to break the news without laughing in the face of Henry's fancy lady with clicky shoes.

But everything he'd planned to say vanished at the sight of the young woman standing in the office, frowning at a metal print of a tractor.

Shelley Powell.

She was absolutely beautiful: tall and elegant, with touchable, tousled blond hair, and she was dressed to impress, with a perfectly smooth straight knee-length skirt and a slinky, low-cut shirt under an open jacket that left very little of the curves of her generous breasts to imagination.

She turned back to the counter, already starting to say, "I'm here about the Lincoln—"

Silver eyes met his and if Dean had thought she was beautiful a moment before, now he was utterly enraptured.

His bear woke within him a start. *She's ours*, he demanded. *Ours forever.*

I wish this for you, Deirdre had told him when she left. *With all my soul, I want you to feel this, to know what it's like.*

At the time, still nurturing the heart she'd broken, Dean had vehemently denied that it was anything he wanted.

Now, he couldn't imagine anything he wanted *more.*

This woman was his *mate.*

She was gazing at him from the most beautiful, wide eyes he'd ever seen, her brilliant red lips perfectly parted in shock.

She knows, Dean realized.

It wasn't just a look of interest, it was a look of recognition, of instant understanding.

It was interest, too, Dean thought breathlessly, and it was decidedly mutual.

Her father was a lion shifter, and her nephew was, too; shifting wasn't something that always bred true, but it wouldn't be too crazy to assume she was one also.

"The... car..."

Dean had to grin, he couldn't help himself. "There's nothing wrong with it," he said apologetically. "It was just a loose license plate."

CHAPTER 5

*S*helley had never spent much time thinking about weddings and true love and making babies like other girls. Wedding *dresses*, because she'd always loved fashion, but the whole idea of waiting around for the perfect guy only made her roll her eyes.

She hadn't even believed in mates until her father introduced her to his, and later casually mentioned that Shaun had married his as well. It was too ridiculous to bear.

But here they were, and her lioness was growling with avid recognition, leaving no doubt in Shelley's mind that *this* was her destiny, *this* was her mate.

If she had ever bothered to imagine meeting her mate, it would not have been like this.

She was sweaty and disheveled from having to walk to the diner, and she'd gotten unexpectedly caught in the arc of a sprinkler on her way back, so her jacket had water spots and her hair was limp.

And the most gorgeous man she'd ever laid eyes on had

just looked straight into her soul and was explaining to her that she was the biggest idiot in the entire sad state.

"The... license plate?" she repeated. "The noise from my car was just a *loose license plate*?"

"That's all it was, ma'am," he said, gazing back at her in a way that would have been creepy if it had been anyone else... or if she had not been staring back at him with equal avarice. "The bolts were loose and that's the rattle you were hearing when you went over bumps. I... tightened them for you."

"Not ma'am," Shelley squeaked. She didn't want to be 'ma'am' to this man. "Shelley." It sounded like a kid's name to her ears. "Michelle." Ugh, no, too formal. "Shelley. Shelley Powell." She realized that he probably already knew her name, since she'd left it with her car key.

She was not doing much to redeem her image of intelligence.

"I'm Dean," he answered, and he offered her a hand. "Dean James, not to be mistaken for James Dean."

Shelley laughed breathlessly. Dean could certainly have been a movie star, with his broad shoulders and strong jaw. She very slowly took his hand to shake and was instantly lost.

If his gaze had left her knees feeling boneless, his handshake did things to parts not much higher, and her chest was suddenly too small for her lungs. She was dizzy, and excited, and... she was ready for this. This was coming home. Her lion was rumbling in delight.

"So, you're..." she started, just as he blushed beautifully and said, "I guess..."

"You first," she said swiftly, and by virtue of her speed, he was forced to continue.

"Are you... a... ah... lion shifter like your nephew and

your father?" he said with understandable hesitation. Being wrong about an assumption like that in a world where shifters were secret would have been a stunning mistake to bring up aloud.

But *this* wasn't a mistake. He was clearly feeling the same thing, the same crazy, perfect, stomach-dropping realization she was tumbling through. He was drinking in her gaze just as she was his, and they hadn't let go of each other after the handshake. Their clasped hands hung just above the countertop. If the counter had not been between them, Shelley was not sure what they would be doing now, but she would bet that it would start with a kiss from those amazing lips, and once the thought occurred to her, she couldn't shake it.

"I am," she finally remembered to confirm, because it seemed impossible that there was anything he didn't know about her. "And… you?"

"Bear," Dean said faintly, like he was imagining the same kiss. "I'm… a bear. Grizzly."

It was the stupidest conversation, dragged out a stupid amount of time, because Shelley couldn't keep a thought in her head that wasn't kissing this man. "I'm a lawyer," she said impulsively, then thought it sounded like she was bragging and blushed. "I mean… I just don't want you to think I'm an idiot. Because of the… license plate."

"Happens all the time," Dean lied kindly.

"You're just being nice," Shelley told him suspiciously.

"Yeah," Dean agreed with a smile.

"Do I owe you anything?"

"No, no charge for tightening your… license plate."

They were still clasping hands over the greasy counter.

"I'm never going to live this down, am I?" Shelley guessed sheepishly.

"It'll be one of those inside jokes that we have."

"You mean, it will actually be funny someday, instead of just horribly humiliating?"

"I promise," Dean breathed.

There was a moment of silence, then they both tried to say, "So, you're…"

This time Dean was fastest. "You first."

"You're my mate," Shelley said boldly. It was thrilling to her own ears. This beautiful man, with his strong hands and his piercing eyes: he was *hers*.

His grin was like a bolt of lightning. "That's what I was going to say," he said.

"It's… it's nice to meet you," Shelley said. Nice was so insufficient! "I… would you like to get dinner or something?" Dinner was the last thing she wanted to do with this man; she wanted to wrap herself around him and see if he tasted the way she was imagining.

She let go of his hand, but only because he was coming around the counter, and she would finally be able to…

"Daddy! Daddy!"

Shelley stumbled backwards instead of taking the step forward that she had intended.

A curly-haired boy about the same age as Trevor bolted into the room like a whirlwind, smelling like leaves and mud puddles. He just missed crashing into Shelley's legs, careening around her and wrapping himself around Dean possessively as the man bent and intercepted his hug.

Shelley stared in horror.

"You… have a kid?" she said hesitantly.

"This is my son, Aaron."

Everything about the mood had changed. Dean was bristling protectively, his arms around the little boy, his gaze challenging.

18

Shelley felt like someone had just hit her in the face, and she probably looked like it, too.

Her mate... had a kid.

Every brief, delirious fantasy she'd had about a life with Dean suddenly had a four-foot-high *nope* in the middle of it.

CHAPTER 6

*D*ean's heart was somewhere near the pit of his stomach.

He hadn't missed the whiplash-fast change in Shelley—in his mate. Aaron's entrance had turned what had been a moment of discovery and delight into something so stiff and awkward that Dean wondered that he was looking at the same woman.

Shelley's look of horror had faded behind a mask of distant disdain, and she was smoothing her jacket as if Aaron had somehow mussed it with his breakneck entrance.

Dean could actually *feel* the dismay radiating from her.

"How was your day at school?" he asked.

"It was only a half-day," Aaron scoffed. "Like Kindergarten for babies. It was stupid but I liked the games and we learned about *mold* and Trevor said a bad word and Clara fell down and skinned her knee and I'm *starving*."

It was, as usual, a moment before Dean could get a word in edgewise. "I brought granola bars," he said.

"The healthy kind?" Aaron asked skeptically, letting go

of him at last. "I like the kind that Trevor gets with the chocolate chips."

"You get what you get—" Dean reminded him, standing up again.

"—And you don't throw a fit," Aaron sighed. But he also muttered defiantly, "I still like Trevor's better."

Dean was keenly aware of Shelley, watching them. She had backed up another step, as if she was afraid that Aaron had something contagious, and was playing with the buttons on her jacket nervously.

He didn't want her any less than he had before Aaron had interrupted them—his bear was still growling inappropriate suggestions in his ear—but the rest of him was in a whirlwind of protective instinct.

It didn't matter what his bear or his body said, she clearly considered Aaron a deal-breaker, and the only thing that Dean could do with that was watch her walk away before they got more invested.

"Your car is ready to go," he said, as coldly as he could manage.

"Thank you for fixing my... er... license plate," she replied, in exactly the same chilly, polite tone.

"Any time."

There was a moment of stiff silence broken only by Aaron rummaging behind the counter for the promised granola bar.

"My key," Shelley finally said, just as Dean said, "Sorry, you'll need your key." It was sitting on the far side of the counter.

He went behind the counter, stepping over Aaron, who was trying to put *all* the granola bars in his pockets, and handed it over to Shelley.

She had to take a step closer, and she held her hand

below it so that Dean could drop it into her palm with risking any brush of skin.

Dean's bear protested, but Dean let the key go, just as Aaron suddenly stood up, his mouth full of granola bar. "You're Trevor's niece!" he exclaimed, spewing crumbs onto the counter.

"Aunt," Shelley corrected, stepping back quickly with her key clutched in her hand. "He's my *nephew*."

Aaron started to slurp his spewed crumbs off the counter and Dean was still watching Shelley's face as she realized he was going to eat off the dirty surface.

"Let's toss those, kiddo," he suggested swiftly.

Aaron made a face, but let Dean sweep them off the counter into his hand and drop them into the trash can.

When Dean looked up again, Shelley was still standing there, face unreadable, keys held so tightly in her hand that they must be biting into her palm.

It suddenly struck him that it wasn't *only* dismay that he was feeling from her. There was dismay, yes, and regret, and surprise, all in a knot of chaotic emotion. And underneath it all... fear.

She was afraid of... Aaron?

This was confirmed when Aaron went out from around the counter, staring at her, and she took an involuntary step back and shot Dean a quick, panicked look.

"Trevor and I are in a SECRET club," Aaron told her. "It's SECRET. I can't tell you about it."

"Didn't you *just* tell me about it?" Shelley said scathingly.

Aaron considered this.

Dean was torn between wanting to throw her out of his shop and out of his life and wanting to laugh hysterically. "Hey Aaron, can you go hang out in the store for just a second? I need to talk to Trevor's aunt."

"Okay!" Aaron said cheerfully. "Bye, Trevor's aunt!"

He tripped away through the door, holding all the extra granola bars in his over-laden pockets.

"I'm sorry," Shelley said hastily. "I'm... not... good with kids. It's not... I mean, I don't hate babies or anything. I just..."

"You're afraid of kids," Dean finished when she couldn't.

He felt unexpectedly sorry for her, with her perfect outfit and her perfect hair, and the way she was fighting to keep her expression calm when he could feel how much fear she was hiding underneath her smooth demeanor.

"They terrify me," Shelley admitted. "Someone gave me a baby yesterday and I nearly cried. I'd be a terrible mom. Or step-mom. Not that I'm suggesting marriage, that's crazy. Oh my god, are you married?"

Dean couldn't keep the wince from his own face and he knew that Shelley would assume the worst, so he hastened to explain, "No, not any more. Divorced. Five years."

Five godawful years, pretending he was heart-whole because he couldn't bear to hurt the woman who'd destroyed his happiness.

"Good," Shelley said crisply. "I mean, not good that you... I mean... this is complicated enough already."

Dean got the impression that she wasn't used to this kind of complication.

"Dinner," he reminded her. "Do you want to try dinner?"

Shelley looked at him and a grateful smile cracked the ivory of the mask she was still trying to settle over her features. "Yes," she said quietly.

"Me and Aaron," Dean said firmly. "We're a package deal."

The smile froze in place, but she nodded anyway. "Is there a good place in town we can go?"

"Neutral ground?" Dean said, unable to keep from teasing.

The smile twitched back into life. "Neutral ground," she agreed.

"Gran's Grits is really the only place in town," Dean said. "It's over past the post office at the corner across from the Presbyterian church."

"It's not hard to find things in this town," Shelley observed. "Tonight?"

"Six okay? I like to get Aaron in bed by eight."

Shelley nodded. Was she blushing? "Six," she said faintly, and then she nodded and smiled and Dean was positive she was blushing and it was absolutely adorable.

"Six," he echoed. "See you then."

"See you then," she said softly, and for one beautiful moment Dean thought he might get the kiss he'd been imagining since they met.

Then she cast a nervous look at the door to the shop and her face went abruptly careful and polite. She gave a crisp nod. Then her feet were clicking away over the floor and the door to the office was shutting behind her and Dean felt like the whole world had suddenly lost a lightbulb.

CHAPTER 7

"*B*ad news about the car?" Tawny asked, opening the door for Shelley. "And you're our guest, you don't have to knock."

"Except on the bedroom door!" Shelley's father, Damien, called from the living room.

Tawny gave a smirk completely at odds with her 'sweet old lady' image. "Yes," she agreed. "That's probably a good idea."

"Oh, gross," Shelley said, following Tawny into the house. "I assure you, I have no desire to barge into your bedroom."

"What's wrong with the car, Shelley?" Damien asked.

"Nothing," Shelley said shortly. "It was just..." the most humiliating introduction to her mate that she could ever have imagined. "Would it be okay if I stayed a few more days?"

"Of course," Tawny said immediately.

"Why?" Damien demanded.

Shelley gave him a much more successful stoneface

than she had managed with Dean. "I just need to figure some things out," she said vaguely.

Her father wasn't fooled, but his return frown was a poor shadow of what a scowl would have been from him before Tawny had taken the reins of his heart. "Are you in some kind of trouble?" he asked at once. "Is it money? Does the car need repairs?"

"It's not money and the car is fine," Shelley snarled back at him, stung. "I'm not a *kid*, Dad."

She stalked away to the kitchen, hoping that filling her empty stomach would make some dent in the hunger that Dean had awakened in her.

The kitchen had nothing to tempt her, and Shelley found herself caught in familiar patterns of thought.

She wasn't the staggering billionaire that her father was, or even the successful millionaire that her brother Shaun was, but she'd done fine for herself; she was a successful contract negotiator for a major engineering firm and there were contractors and lawyers that trembled at the sound of her name. In some circles she was known as Shelley the Shark. She was on track for a comfortable early retirement, and had a luxurious standard of living. She was doing *great*.

On the outside.

The bottle of pills in her purse said otherwise.

What would those lawyers think if they knew that Shelley the Shark was toothless? She had them all fooled into thinking she was powerful and fearless, when the truth was the exact opposite.

She was broken inside, constantly fighting thoughts of doubt and self-hatred. Her logical mind, so good at unraveling legal issues and finding weaknesses in contract language, seemed to relish pointing out to herself all the ways she'd failed, all her blunders, every stupid statement.

She only got where she was by playing on her looks, only succeeded because other people let her, only frightened people because they didn't know how fearful she actually was.

Her mate knew, she thought, feeling her chest tighten warningly. Her mate had seen her make a complete idiot out of herself, watched her flinch from a child. *His* child.

How could he possibly still want her?

Tawny found her standing in front of the open refrigerator staring sightlessly at the shelves.

"Here, sit down," Tawny told her with a tone of amused tolerance. "I'll whip you up a little snack and you can tell me why you suddenly want to spend extra time in a town that smells like cows."

Shelley sat at the little kitchen table obediently. "Tawny... when you met my Dad...?" She didn't know how to finish the sentence she'd started.

Tawny gave her a knowing look. "Did you meet someone?" she asked.

"Dean," Shelley breathed, without meaning to. It was his grin that she remembered most, white teeth in that tanned face.

Tawny laughed. "Green Valley's most eligible divorcee," she said approvingly. "You wouldn't be the first to fall for that handsome face and broken heart."

Such a handsome face. "Wait, broken heart?"

Tawny put a plate down in front of her: sliced cheese, fresh bread, and a tidy pile of vegetable fingers, including carrots. Plain fare, but it seemed like just the right thing. Shelley took a nibble of cheese as Tawny sat opposite from her.

"Dean James married his high school sweetheart, Deirdre, not long after they both graduated. They... were young. I won't say the marriage was perfect, but they cared for each other, and they had a darling little boy about five years later."

"Aaron," Shelley said, surprised to find that she had finished the slice of cheese. "We met."

"When Aaron was about two, Deirdre left Dean for another man."

Shelley promptly hated Deirdre and took a savage bite of the bread.

"Dean put a really good face on it; the divorce was completely amicable, and they share custody. He never lets anyone say a word against her, or the man she left him for, and to all appearances, they're all friends. But the light... sort of went out of him when it happened."

Shelley blinked at her, trying to resolve Dean as someone the light had gone out of. He was *all* light, with that amazing smile and those hazel eyes.

"Every eligible woman in Green Valley and a whole lot of women who aren't even slightly eligible have offered to be Aaron's new mom, believe me," Tawny said.

And there was the rub.

"I would *not* be a good mom."

Tawny blinked at her. "You're thinking that seriously about him?" Understanding dawned in her eyes. "Oh, honey, is he your mate?"

Shelley's lioness gave a yearning rumble and Shelley didn't answer Tawny, only looked down at her plate of food without appetite for it.

"I don't want kids," Shelley said miserably, rolling a cherry tomato around on her plate. "I never did. You saw me with Patricia's baby, I'm hopeless! How can someone so right for me be so completely wrong?"

"Well, kids aren't babies," Tawny pointed out. "Aaron's a little past bottles or needing diapers changed."

"He's still a kid," Shelley pointed out. "In his formative

years, and all. I don't want to screw that up. I have tons of terrible habits and I don't know the first thing about small people or what to do with them." Shelley thought longingly of the pills in her purse. She could feel the tightness in her chest, and the way that breaths didn't feel quite deep enough, her mind already in familiar spirals.

"No parent ever does," Tawny assured her. "Everyone who's ever had a baby has been dumped feet-first into I-have-no-idea-what-I'm-doing soup. All you can do is muddle through and love them."

"What if I *can't* love him?" Shelley asked desperately. "What if I never even like him? What if *he* hates *me*? Dean won't want to have anything to do with me if I can't do that... nurturing mom crap, and I don't know if I have that in me. Maybe I was just born without it. Maybe I'm... broken."

Tawny was laughing, and it was a warm, non-judgmental laugh. "You're not broken," she assured Shelley. She reached over and stole a carrot from the edge of Shelley's plate. "I never particularly wanted children, either. There was a period I went through where I sort of mourned *not* having them, but I wasn't really sure if I was just regretting that I hadn't followed the usual patterns of love and marriage and kids. And now I've got you and Shaun, and your father, and I have never been more sure that my life unfolded exactly as it was supposed to."

"I'm twenty-seven," Shelley pointed out. "That's a far cry from suddenly having a kid who is *seven*."

"All the same rules apply," Tawny pointed out. "You listen when they talk to you and you learn to love them, because they came from something that you already love."

Her smile across the table was direct and Shelley felt an involuntary swell of affection that seemed to loosen the band around her chest. She squirmed, as uncomfortable with topics of emotion as she was with children. "I... I don't know if I love him," she said hastily. "I just met him. And oh... he must think I'm a complete idiot."

"I don't think first impressions are everything," Tawny advised her. "Your father dumped a potluck plate down my shirt when we met and then made a little kid cry."

"Remember the sound I took the car in for?" Shelley asked. "The sound I thought was the shocks or something? It was a loose license plate. Dean had to look me in the eyes and tell me that he tightened the *license plate* bolts for me."

Tawny stared at her for a moment, then burst out laughing. "A... loose license plate?"

"He must think I'm a complete moron," Shelley said in despair. "And then I acted like his son was... a plague bearer or something."

"Fortunately, being seven is not contagious," Tawny said drolly. "What are you going to do next?"

"Dinner," Shelley said, eating the last of the tomatoes from her plate. All that remained now were the detested carrots. "I have to go to that dreadful little diner with the plastic bench seats and try to redeem myself over gravy-laden, greasy spoon food."

"Gran's Grits may not have the oversized square plates with the fancy drizzles," Tawny said, rather severely. "But they serve good hearty food that will fill your belly at a decent price, and you'll sleep well knowing that you've helped support one of the pillars of our community."

It was as close to a scold as Tawny had ever given her, and Shelley was instantly abashed. "You're right," she said as graciously as she could. "I will keep that in mind."

Tawny softened. "Just keep your heart open," she suggested, rising and taking Shelley's plate with the disdained carrots to the counter.

Shelley rose, too. She needed a long, hot shower. And a different wardrobe. And to be a different person. She paused at the doorway. "Thanks, Tawny," she said sincerely.

Tawny's smile was brilliant. "Trust your instincts," she said gently.

But Shelley couldn't tell what was instinct and what was terror.

CHAPTER 8

*I*t was everything that Dean could do to keep from fidgeting, playing with the menu that he already had memorized, the glasses of ice water, the napkins.

"Why are we having dinner with Trevor's niece?" Aaron wanted to know.

"Trevor's aunt," Dean corrected. "Shelley's brother is Trevor's dad."

"Oh," Aaron said, but he was undeterred. "Why are we having dinner with her?"

"Because I like her," Dean said, not at all sure how to explain something he wasn't at all sure about.

"Does she like you?" Aaron asked avidly.

"I think so," Dean said. But he knew that *he* wasn't the problem, and he certainly wasn't going to explain to his son that Shelley was dubious about the baggage that he came with. He would never let Aaron think he was baggage.

"Is this a date?" Aaron asked, disgust on his face. He had something on his chin and Dean dipped a napkin into his water glass and tried to scrub it off. "Are you going to kiss?" Aaron asked skeptically, trying to squirm away.

"It's just dinner," Dean said, triumphant over the… whatever it had been on his son's face.

But the thought of kissing Shelley was deeply disturbing, and he was still helplessly thinking about it when the door to the diner gave a tinkle.

Andrea was bringing him a new napkin, and she looked over to the entrance.

"Hey Shelley," Andrea called loudly. "Dean's over here!"

"Thanks, Andrea," Dean hissed at her.

"Any time, Sausage." Andrea grinned at him knowingly, entirely too amused by the entire situation.

Dean didn't think that she guessed Shelley was his mate, she was just enjoying the novelty of seeing him out with someone, and was entertained by the idea that Shaun's prim sister would date a rough-edged mechanic like him.

Then he edged out of the booth to greet Shelley and got lost in her silver eyes.

She was tall to start with and with her heels on—who wore heels to a diner like Gran's?—she looked directly into his face. Everything about her said that she didn't belong here: her glamorous make-up, her designer blouse, her seductively short skirt, her perfectly highlighted hair.

And everything inside of him said that she did belong here, with him, in his arms.

"Hi," she said, as breathlessly as if she was somehow as enamored with him as he was with her. Dean realized that he'd been staring at her for several moments and wasn't sure how he was supposed to proceed.

Aaron climbed into the bench seat behind him. "Are you going to kiss my Dad?" he asked point-blank.

Dean winced. "Aaron…"

But Shelley gave a crooked smile that looked like she didn't practice it as much as her frown or her serene mask. "It's a valid question." She looked past Dean to where Aaron was kneeling on the bench seat. "Do you want me to?"

"Oh, gross, no, ew!" Aaron keeled over on the bench, pretending to throw up and spasm in disgust. Laughter from the few other tables that were occupied only encouraged his antics. "Yuck, yuck, YUCK."

"Okay, that's enough," Dean said, embarrassed. He sat down next to Aaron and pushed him over on the bench. "Restaurant manners," he reminded the boy.

Shelley sat gracefully across from them. The crooked smile had been replaced by a perfect company smile, but her eyes on Aaron were deeply skeptical.

Aaron gave one last seizure of disapproval and to Dean's relief, chose to sit up in his seat rather than test his audience. They'd had a long talk about manners before they left the house, but Dean wasn't sure how seriously he was taking this.

Andrea brought a glass of ice water and a straw for Shelley. "Thank you," Shelley said gravely, and she fastidiously tore off the end of the wrapper and pulled out the straw, leaving a perfect paper tunnel behind.

Is that what she would do to him? Dean wondered poetically. Would she decide that a mate with a child wasn't what she was looking for and walk away with his heart?

And when had he given her his heart?

Dammit.

"Can I get you started with some drinks?" Andrea asked, all innocence.

"Diet cola," Shelley said.

"Can I have a pop?" Aaron asked, voice treacherously close to a whine.

"Too close to bedtime, sorry. Do you want a glass of milk?"

"I want a pop," Aaron said stubbornly.

Keenly aware of Shelley's neutral expression from across the table and Andrea's amused observation, Dean asked, "Do you want milk, or just water?"

"Milk," Aaron sulked, to his relief.

"Just water for me," Dean told Andrea.

"Coming up, Sausage!"

"Sausage?" Shelley asked, once Andrea had left. "What's that about?" Her glance flickered nervously to Aaron, as if she was afraid she'd asked a question that she shouldn't have in front of him.

"It's... a stupid name thing," Dean said, embarrassed. "Andrea and I went to high school together when we were kids. Dean James, James Dean, Jimmy Dean... the brand of sausage. That was the one that had to stick."

Shelley looked amused.

"We're not supposed to use the word stupid," Aaron reminded him, still pouting about the pop.

"You're right," Dean told him. "Sorry about that."

Shelley played nervously with her water while Dean dredged for a topic that would work for the three of them.

"Did you have fun at school today?" Shelley asked Aaron before Dean could come up with anything.

"Yeah," Aaron said with a shrug.

"What's your favorite topic?" she asked into the unhelpful silence he left her. She was trying so hard.

Aaron shrugged again. "Recess, I guess."

"You like math," Dean prodded him.

"Yeah."

It would have been an awkward silence if it weren't for

Andrea's arrival with their drinks. Shelley looked at her gratefully. "Thank you."

Aaron muttered his thanks after Dean reminded him, and proceeded to make a paper rocket ship from his straw wrapper.

"Have you decided what to order?" Andrea asked. "Or do you need a little more time?"

"I'll take the special," Shelley said demurely.

Dean glanced at the sticky note on the menu. Shelley didn't seem like the chicken fried steak type, but maybe she would surprise him.

"Corn dogs!" Aaron chorused, holding up his half-colored paper menu. "Fries! Lots of ketchup!"

"I'll take the special, too," Dean decided.

Andrea took their laminated menus. "Be about ten minutes," she said cheerfully.

CHAPTER 9

*T*his whole thing was a terrible mistake, Shelley decided.

The date, the diner, the clothes she'd picked out, the fact that her mate had a kid…

But most of all, the chicken fried steak.

After closer to fifteen minutes of awkward conversation dominated by Aaron's nearly-indecipherable but very enthusiastic explanations about something called Minecraft (Shelley guessed it was a cartoon she wasn't familiar with), Andrea brought her a steaming plate… of gravy.

A cautious poke revealed a sublayer of some kind of deep-fried meat, and there was a side of hashbrowns completely submerged in the lumpy cream-colored goo.

Keenly aware of the scrutiny she was under from what felt like the entire diner, Shelley sawed off a tiny piece of the mystery meat and prepared for the worst, already practicing her best smile and pretend enjoyment. She was *not* going to be the snobbish *prima donna* she knew that everyone must think she was; she was going to choke down the greasy food like it was ambrosia from heaven for polite-ness sake.

Dean was busy trying to keep Aaron from upsetting his milk onto his plate as the little boy poured half a bottle of ketchup over his fries.

Shelley put the bite into her mouth... and was pleas-antly relieved to find that it was nowhere near the flavor or texture she was expecting. The lumps in the smooth gravy were little pieces of sausage, popping with flavor, and the meat had been tenderized into something far more chew-able than she had feared. The breading was a neutral layer that perfectly complemented the rest.

A tentative taste showed that the hashbrowns were just as good; fried crispy but not soaked in oil.

Shelley looked up and accidentally met Dean's eyes.

"Like it?" he asked, a smile twitching at his mouth.

"Yeah," Shelley said honestly. Did she sound too surprised? "It's really good."

"Old George is the best short order cook in a hundred miles," Dean said with satisfaction. "Gran's Grits may not have the fanciest menu, but what they serve is always great."

He reminded Aaron not to talk with his mouth full of food and took a generous bite from his own plate.

As good as the food had turned out to be, Shelley was suddenly hungry for something else altogether.

He was so handsome, and every move he made was graceful and strong. Shelley had never considered eating particularly sexy until she was watching him draw a fork from between his lips, and she had to blink carefully and make herself eat several mechanical bites before she could look up and meet his eyes.

Those hazel eyes were dancing again and Shelley real-ized with chagrin that he knew exactly what he'd done to her. His next bite was deliberately slow and he actually licked his lips afterwards.

Shelley knew a challenge when she saw one, and two could play that game. Her next bite was just as slow as his, and she closed her eyes and gave a little shiver of pleasure.

"Glad to see you're enjoying your meal," Andrea said, and Shelley's eyes flew open as her cheeks turned scarlet.

"My… uh… compliments to your chef," Shelley said in a squeak.

"Can I get you guys anything?" Andrea asked drolly. "Like, a room?"

"More milk!" Aaron said enthusiastically, thankfully oblivious to anything else happening at the table. Somehow his plate was already mostly empty.

"How do you ask?" Dean reminded him, still grinning at Shelley.

"MayIpleasehavemoremilk?" Aaron asked.

"I'm good," Shelley said faintly.

"I'll be right back with another milk," Andrea said cheerfully.

Shelley continued to eat her food trying not to meet Dean's eyes because every time she did, they both broke into laughter… much to the mystification of Aaron.

"What's funny?" he finally asked, around a mouthful of fries. "I don't get it."

"You will someday," Dean told him.

To her own surprise, Shelley finished her entire plate, wiping up the delicious gravy with her toast. She usually tried to eat light, and often found heavy food like this too much to finish.

"Dessert?" Andrea offered.

"I couldn't…" Shelley said just as Aaron stuffed his final bit of corndog in his mouth and declared, "I ate all my food canIhaveabrownie?"

"Chew and swallow, kiddo," Dean told him.

Aaron did so, obediently, then politely asked, "Could I can I may I have a brownie?"

"Please," Dean whispered sideways.

"PLEASE."

"One brownie?" Andrea confirmed.

"Make it two," Dean said magnanimously.

Andrea took their plates and the half-dozen crumpled napkins that Aaron had managed to generate.

"Thanks for coming out with us," Dean said, almost shyly. How could someone look so heart-bendingly adorable and so undeniably masculine at the same time?

"Thanks for inviting me," Shelley said, feeling just as shy. "I've had a really good time."

She had, she realized.

Aaron had been disruptive and there were several times she had wondered exactly how he could pack that much food into such a small mouth and still try talking. But he… was kind of cute, she supposed, and he at least made an attempt at manners; it was hard to dislike something that was so *happy* and trying so hard. And the food was much better than she had expected; her stomach felt comfortably full and warm.

The brownies that Andrea brought were served warm, with ice cream, and Aaron dove into his with enthusiasm, nearly unseating his ice cream scoop in his attempt to cut the brownie with his fork.

"Want to try a bite?" Dean offered Shelley, holding out a square of warm chocolate draped in melting ice cream at the end of a fork.

Shelley couldn't figure out how to say no, and she didn't really want to, so she leaned forward and opened her mouth.

Feeding someone else was supposed to be something

seductive and sexy, and this might have been the kind of moment a younger Shelley might have written about in her journal, dripping with purple prose.

Instead, Aaron dropped his current bite of brownie directly into his lap with a loud yelp of surprise, startling Dean into veering off from Shelley's mouth and he stabbed the brownie he was offering directly into her cheek instead. The soft brownie disintegrated and the ice cream coated crumbs dropped straight down Shelley's cleavage.

CHAPTER 10

*S*helley gave a squeak of dismay as Dean tried to rise to offer a napkin and bumped the table, nearly toppling Aaron's milk. "I got it, I got it," she protested, trying to fish the pieces out of her shirt.

Aaron howled in laughter, and Dean chuckled and tried to clean up his son's lap while trying very hard not to stare as Shelley, embarrassed and laughing helplessly, mined into her shirt.

"This is going to take a bathroom visit," she finally admitted sheepishly. She gathered up her purse and clicked off in her heels like a runway model and Dean watched her go helplessly.

"Why are her shoes like that?" Aaron asked, his laughter finally fading. They were the last people eating in the diner and the sound of her steps was very loud in the quiet little room.

"They're just fancy," Dean said. Everything about Shelley was fancy. "Do you… like her?"

Aaron considered the question as he put his last bite of brownie into his mouth. "She's okay," he decided.

Dean's bear wanted to protest that she was much more than okay. She was beautiful and elegant and she was trying so hard to look like she wasn't completely out of her element. She listened to Aaron's monologues patiently, even if she looked utterly confused by them, and she was polite and gracious.

And when she laughed…

When she laughed, Dean could see straight through into her joyous heart, and he loved what he saw there unreservedly.

"She's kind of… funny," Aaron declared.

Andrea brought the check and Dean opened his wallet and gave her a credit card. "How'd the date go, Sausage?"

"It wasn't a date," Aaron said with authority. "It was just dinner."

Dean cast a glance at the bathroom, but there was no sign of Shelley yet. "It went fine," he said briefly. "Thanks."

"Are you going to kiss her?" Aaron asked again, fortunately waiting until Andrea had gone to run the credit card.

Dean looked thoughtfully back at him. "Would you mind if I did?" he asked.

Aaron dragged his fork through the melted ice cream on his plate, considering. Finally, he shrugged. "It would be okay."

Shelley's heels gave ample warning across the linoleum floor, and by the time she had returned to the table, Dean had gotten Aaron into his jacket and pulled his own on.

Taking the cue, Shelley put down her purse and put her own jacket on. Dean tried not to gaze foolishly at her. Had she put new makeup on in the bathroom? She looked like she was straight out of a magazine, almost distractingly perfect.

"Don't forget your credit card!" Andrea called.

Dean signed the receipt, left a tip in cash, and the three of them walked out into the darkness.

"I, ah, drove," Shelley pointed out. Hers was the only car in front of the diner.

"We walked," Aaron volunteered. "We live right over there."

"This is goodbye, then," Shelley said nervously. "Ah… thanks again for tightening my license plate. Next time I should get dinner. If there… is…"

"I'd like to see you again," Dean said swiftly.

They were standing very close on the narrow sidewalk. Aaron had walked a few steps away and was kicking a rustling drift of leaves. Dean closed the distance between them before he could lose his nerve, putting a hand on Shelley's face and bending forward to kiss her with his bear leaning on him avidly.

She hesitated, drawing away. "What about Aaron," she whispered. "He didn't…"

"He said it would be okay," Dean assured her, grateful that she cared.

Then she was meeting his mouth with hers and she was in his arms at last… and it was all much more than just *okay*.

He tried to keep it a chaste kiss, a polite first kiss that you'd have in public, knowing that Aaron's weren't the only prying eyes around. Shelley trembled in his embrace, like she was fighting her own instincts, and opened her mouth with a whimper of need.

It wasn't very chaste after that.

Shelley's arms slipped up around his neck, and Dean claimed her mouth with a crushing, probing kiss, cradling her face with one hand, holding her close at the waist with the other. Her whole body pressed up tight to him, in all its gorgeous, curvy perfection, and it still wasn't close enough. He needed her, craved her like a starving man.

"Can we go now?"

Aaron's unimpressed voice dragged him back and Dean reluctantly let go of Shelley and stepped away. She was panting, eyes wide and her cheeks flushed. She licked her lips and swallowed.

"Deirdre's going to be picking up Aaron tomorrow after school. Do you want to come over and have dinner… maybe watch a movie?"

"I want to watch a movie," Aaron said enthusiastically.

Dean definitely didn't, and he watched Shelley realize what he was suggesting. Her silver eyes widened and her breath caught in her throat. "I'd like that," she said softly.

"Can we watch *Iron Man*?" Aaron suggested. "Trevor got to see it already."

"You're going to your mom's," Dean reminded him.

"Will she let me watch *Iron Man*?"

"That's up to her," Dean said. He was still gazing at Shelley, who had turned several interesting colors and was back to flushed. "At six?"

"Six sounds great," she said, and she gave that shy half-smile that Dean was sure she had never practiced, because it was so tentative and real.

Then Aaron took him by the hand and drug him away as Shelley got into her car.

CHAPTER 11

"*Y*ou never used to go out with us," Shelley said skeptically as Damien's car pulled into the parking area at the end of the short drive. "Are you sure this place is safe?"

"Roar!" Trevor said enthusiastically from the back seat. "I'm going to be a lion!"

"Wait!" Damien said severely, ignoring Shelley. "I don't want clawmarks on my seats."

"Yes, Grandpa," Trevor said meekly.

Shelley filed Damien's tone for a time she might need it with Aaron. A few days before, she would have considered an afternoon out with Trevor some kind of torture, but now anything that could help her understand Aaron seemed like a misery worth enduring.

And it had been a *long* while since she'd let her lion out to stretch.

"This is private property," Damien explained. "There shouldn't be anyone else around."

"We're here already?" Trevor said. "Can I get out? Can I change? Can I can I can I?"

"It's so close to town," Shelley said, opening her own door and frowning at the dirty leaves littering the ground. "Aren't you worried someone will wander here by mistake?"

Damien gave her an impatient look. "Do you want to get out, or not?"

Shelley sighed and slipped off her heels. While Damien got Trevor out of the other side of the car, she undressed swiftly and put her clothing neatly in her seat. Then she shifted, and closed the car door with her heavy feline head.

"Now, you think about what it feels like to be a lion," Damien was saying to the little boy. "How it feels to be covered in fur, and walking around on four paws. What your tail feels like, how clear your hearing is."

"Springy!" Trevor said. "It feels springy!"

Quick as a blink, he was flinging himself at the ground and cavorting away as a lion cub.

"Good job!" Damien said warmly. Shelley turned away while he undressed himself and after a moment, there were three lions wandering into the autumn forest.

Her lioness was nearly as tall at the shoulder as her father's thick-maned, silver-touched lion. Trevor, half-grown and tripping over his big paws, still had adolescent spots and barely came to their bellies. He pranced as tall as he could behind them, scampering to chase leaves and bat at low branches.

One of his adventures brought him tumbling into Shelley's legs, and she had to rein back her lioness' instinct to send him rolling away with a cuff from her paw.

We wouldn't hurt him, her lioness insisted. *But you have to keep him in line. Play rough, because the world is hard.*

Even her animal knew more about parenting than she did, Shelley thought bitterly. All she knew was that she was sorely unqualified, and she was terrified of doing it all wrong.

There is no wrong way to do it, her lioness said reassuringly.

Then it's me, Shelley protested. ***I'm*** *wrong. I'm not supposed to be a mom.*

*Our mate has a cub, so you **are** supposed to be.*

Shelley wished she could be as confident as her lioness. She wanted to be with Dean, but she couldn't help wondering if fate had just... messed up on this one. Gotten everything wrong, somehow.

She sat, tail swishing, and watched Damien teach Trevor about stalking and how to step quietly. Shelley was amused to note that Damien had no hesitation about sending him crashing into the brush with one of his big paws when he was getting over-enthusiastic. Trevor simply rolled and bounced back up to attention.

When had Damien picked up parenting? He had always been the absent one when Shelley and Shaun were growing up, as safely distant from the child duties as he could manage to be. He showed up for the requisite concerts and recitals, but it was always with a suffering air, like he couldn't wait to be back to *real* work.

And yet here he was, with Trevor, looking completely comfortable in the role of guide and teacher, and acting surprisingly patient.

A bird caught her attention and Shelley stilled her tail, watching it from the corner of her eye.

She crouched, gauging the distance between them, and the bird flitted a little further away. Shelley froze, and it hopped along its new branch. She was aware of Damien, nudging Trevor to watch, and she moved a step forward in careful slow motion, staying low and gathered.

She sprang without pausing, using her powerful hind legs to drive her into a leap—not at the bird, but at the space above the bird. It rose in terror, and she trapped it between her front paws and landed on her side, rolling onto her back as she fell.

Then she opened her paws, and let the petrified bird, unharmed, fly free.

It scolded her from the safety of a nearby tree.

"Wow!" Trevor exclaimed, standing again as a little boy. "That was amazing! Did you see that Grandpa? It was so cool! I want to do that! Aunt Shelley is incredible!"

Shelley licked her paw casually and Damien gave a cough of humor, staying in lion form.

Trevor looked between them, and fell on all fours… but was still a little boy. He looked down at himself curiously. "I'm not a lion," he pouted.

Shelley twisted back up onto her feet and shook the leaves off of herself while Trevor tried various tricks to get back into lion form. "It's not working!" he complained. "Why isn't it working?"

An idea occurred to Shelley and she walked to where Trevor was standing—and bowled him over with her head.

He bounded to his feet a lion again, making happy loud noises that weren't really roars. Shelley wondered how close they were to Green Valley, and winced when Damien put his head in the air and gave a true lion roar. Doubtlessly someone had heard *that*.

Shelley turned back the way they'd come and heard the others follow: Damien's paws heavy but quiet, Trevor like a small whirlwind through the dry leaves.

Once they had shifted back and dressed, they piled back into the car and returned to Damien's house.

Trevor, full of energy, went with Tawny for a piano lesson.

"Might have been a mistake to wind him up first," Damien admitted as he and Shelley watched them go down the hall to the music room, Trevor making his best— and loudest—lion sounds while Tawny tried to quiz him about his practice time that week.

Shelley shut down her snarky instinct to say *you think?* and just shrugged.

"Shelley…"

Shelley looked at her father and immediately knew that Tawny had already told him about Dean. She braced herself for doubt and anxiety and was surprised and relieved that she didn't feel either.

"Thanks for inviting me out," she said swiftly as she hung up her jacket. "It's been a long time since I was out on four paws and it was nice to stretch."

"Might snow next week," Damien said mildly. "Thought it would be good to get out before we would be leaving too many tracks."

Shelley made a neutral noise of agreement.

"Do you want an apology?" Damien growled unexpectedly.

Shelley returned his scowl. "For what?"

Her father looked desperately uncomfortable behind his customary frown. "I haven't been the greatest role model of parenting."

"I never asked you to be," Shelley said shortly. This wasn't about Dean, this was about *Aaron*.

"But maybe you deserved… better," Damien said stiffly. "I could have been… more involved with your life."

"You mean, like not shipping us off to boarding schools when we got difficult?" Maybe it wasn't about Aaron, either.

"I'm not going to excuse the mistakes I made," Damien said firmly. "I wasn't very present for you and Shaun. I thought someone else could do a better job with you than I could, and I was wrong."

Shelley looked at Damien warily, not sure what to do with an admission of fault from the man who never admitted weakness.

"You kids scared the spit out of me," Damien said honestly.

Shelley knew she was staring openly now, with no control over her face whatsoever, or the tears that were pricking at her eyes.

"I wanted the absolute best for you, and it never occurred to me that what you really needed was just for me to be there for you."

"Dad…"

"I love you, Shelley-bean. And I'm proud of you. And you can do a better job at this than I did."

"You… didn't do a bad job," Shelley choked.

"Of course I didn't," Damien scoffed with a hint of his usual arrogant self. "Look at you! But I could have done a lot of things better and you don't have to go and make the same mistakes." He folded his arms and looked at her severely. "I am *assuming* you aren't going to turn tail and run away from a little problem like this," he challenged.

A little four-foot problem with a snotty nose and the power to strike utter terror into Shelley's heart.

She drew herself up. "Whatever else you did, you didn't raise a coward, Dad," she said fiercely.

"That's my girl."

Impulsively, Shelley stepped forward, and they shared a swift hug. "Thanks, Dad," she murmured into his shoulder, softly enough that he might not hear her. "I love you, too."

Then she straightened and backed away and they exchanged frowns.

"I might not be back tonight," she said frankly.

"I wouldn't expect you to be," Damien agreed. Then he unexpectedly grinned. "If you do come back, you'd better knock. It'll be the first time Tawny and I have the house to ourselves since we got married."

Shelley made a gagging noise. "Oh my god, Dad. No. Too much information. Let's go back to being cold and distant now, please."

He walked away laughing, and Shelley went bemusedly back to her room to change.

This weekend, at least, she could have Dean to herself, the way everything inside of her yearned to have him, and next week she could jump feet-first into I-don't-know-what-I'm-doing soup.

CHAPTER 12

*D*ean paced.

"I'm boooored," Aaron moaned, laying upside down with his feet over the back of the couch. "Can't I watch TV?"

"Your mom should be here at any moment," Dean said, looking at his watch for at least the seventeenth time. "I want you to be ready to go."

"I'll turn it right off," Aaron wheedled. "My bag is already packed, and I've got my shoes on already."

They were indeed on, pointing straight up into the air with shoelaces untied and tongues crooked.

But Dean knew better than to think that Aaron would be able to shut off the television himself without a physical intervention. "She'll be here soon," he growled. He pulled out his phone and looked despairingly at the unread status of the text he'd sent.

It didn't really mean much; Deirdre was constantly letting her phone run out of charge. And it wasn't even that unusual that she was running late. Still, an hour late was into the territory where he was allowed to be a little put-out, wasn't it?

"I'm so booooooored," Aaron repeated. Then he sat up. "I'm hungry! Can I have a snack?"

"Get your shoes off the couch," Dean reminded him. "Yeah, how about…" what was easiest? "A cheese-stick?"

Aaron managed to drag his shoes across nearly the entire couch getting them down to the ground. "Can I have crackers with it?" he begged.

Dean grimaced, dreading the time it would take but unable to come up with a good argument against it. "Let's make you a bag to go," he suggested. "But don't get crumbs in your mom's car."

Aaron danced off to the kitchen merrily and Dean's heart rose up in his chest as he heard a car pull up outside. It was a few minutes before six… Shelley might be early. He ran a hand through his hair and tugged the wrinkles out of his shirt.

"Sorry I'm late!" Deirdre called, walking in as she knocked. "I was a little delayed and then there was construction just outside of Madison."

"Aaron, your mom is here, let's go!"

Dean thrust the bag at Deirdre. "His allergy medicine is in the outside pocket, he's got a page of math home-work, and he says he left his favorite hat at your place so he doesn't need one." His words tumbled out over each other; Dean didn't realize how fast he was talking until he heard himself. "Come on, Aaron!"

Deirdre gave him a puzzled look. "I think I saw his hat at home," she said with a slow nod. "Hi sweetie!"

Aaron had apparently tried to fit the entire box of crackers into a bag, and was now struggling to close it. Bingo trailed behind him hoping for overflow. "Hi Mom! Can you close this for me?"

Deirdre gave him a hug and a kiss on the head, then deftly ate a handful of crackers from the bag so she could close it. "Have a good week, honey?"

"He was great," Dean answered for Aaron. He didn't want to actually shoo them out, and it took all of his self-control to keep from flapping his hands anxiously at them.

Aaron, predictably, started a lengthy, rambling story about something that Trevor had done at school.

"You can tell her in the car, kiddo," Dean said desperately. "Get your hug!"

Aaron took a breath and started part two of his story, tolerating Dean's hug distantly.

"I'll miss you," Dean reminded him.

"Yeah, Dad," Aaron said, returning the hug more sincerely.

"Thanks," Deirdre said cheerfully. "See you on Sunday night," she said as they started down the sidewalk to the curb.

Part three of the tale was unwinding and Dean was ready to close the door when Aaron suddenly turned around. "I don't have my Batman pajamas!"

Dean groaned. "You have your green pajamas," he said hopefully. "Won't those do?"

Aaron stared in horror. "No, I need my Batman pajamas! Otherwise, I might get scared."

"There's nothing scary in your room," Deirdre reminded him with an amused smile.

"I neeeeeeeeeed them!" Aaron insisted.

"I think they're in the hamper," Dean said despairingly.

"We can wash them tomorrow morning," Deirdre said with a shrug to Dean.

"Go get them," Dean said to Aaron, defeated.

Aaron scampered past, shoes flapping. "Wait, wait,"

Dean insisted. "You can't run upstairs with your shoes untied."

He knelt to tie up the shoes and Aaron fidgeted, making the task even harder. "Okay, go," he said at last, and Aaron was off like a shot.

When he stood up, Deirdre was looking at him suspiciously.

"What?" he asked.

"You picked up the house," she observed.

"I do that, from time to time," Dean said defensively.

"You also got a haircut," she pointed out.

"I do that periodically, too," Dean said, resisting his urge to run his fingers through it again.

"I'm sorry I was late," she said, eyes narrow. "It's not usually a big deal."

"It's fine," Dean growled. "Aaron, did you *find* them?" he called.

"You're trying pretty hard to get rid of us," Deirdre pointed out.

"Trevor's niece is coming over!" Aaron hollered, appearing at the top of the stairs. "They're going to watch a movie, can I watch *Iron Man*?"

"Trevor's…?"

"Aunt," Dean groaned. "Trevor's *aunt*. Shaun's sister."

Comprehension dawned in Deirdre's face. "Oh my God, Dean, you have a *date*, that's *great*!"

"Aaron, are you ready to go?" Dean begged.

Bingo, hearing the word *go*, barked in excitement.

And that's when Shelley pulled up.

CHAPTER 13

*I*t wasn't like Shelley dated a lot, but she wasn't a nun, either. She knew what to expect from a second date, especially on the heels of a first date and a kiss like Dean's.

But when she pulled up to Dean's house, nothing was the way she had expected it to be.

Shelley had to sit in the car a moment and screw up her courage to get out when she realized that Aaron was still there... and worse yet, a woman who must be Deirdre, standing in the open door.

She put her chin high as she stepped out, and tugged her skirt down into place. This was undoubtedly going to be ugly. Deirdre, Tawny had said, had broken Dean's heart. That wasn't the kind of thing that left emotions unruffled. And she was the new woman in Dean's life, she reminded herself. Maybe. Hopefully?

Two steps up the sidewalk, a dog came barking to greet her: a large, slobbering, brown and white mutt with floppy ears that immediately tried to jump up and lick her face.

"Nice doggy!" Shelley squeaked, trying to push it down

and keep her purse out of its reach and not fall over, all at once. Why wasn't it afraid of her lion?

"Bingo! Bingo down! Bingo leave it!" Dean came running to her rescue, pulling the dog down and ruffling its ears affectionately as it wiggled in joy.

"You have a *dog*," Shelley observed brilliantly, further cementing the impression of intelligence that she'd started with.

"His name is Bingo," Dean said, looking sheepish. "Aaron named him. Like the kid's song, you know. B-I-N-G-O."

Was it a dig on the fact that she knew nothing about kids? "I remember that song," she said tightly.

"He's a goon, sorry."

"It's fine," Shelley said faintly as they closed the distance to his porch. Clearly, her mate starter-kit came with everything: an old farmhouse, a dog, a kid... and a gorgeous ex-wife who'd broken his heart.

Deirdre was effortlessly beautiful, in a sunny, country way, with curly brown hair highlighted golden and big blue eyes.

She even had adorable freckles, scattered all over her cheeks and nose.

She beamed at Shelley rather alarmingly, and immediately offered her a hand to shake. "I'm Deirdre," she greeted. "Aaron's mom."

"It's nice to meet you," Shelley said, hoping she didn't sound as chilly to Deirdre as she did to her own ears. She reminded herself to smile.

The handshake was swift and utilitarian and Shelley wondered if the glance that Deirdre gave Dean wasn't a little skeptical.

They had the mannerisms of people who were used to talking to each other without words, who knew each other so well that they were having an entire conversation with eyebrows and angles of the shoulder while Shelley stood there feeling left out and out-classed, even in her custom-altered designer clothes, with her name-brand purse and $300 shoes.

Even the dog, Bingo, had decided that she was no longer new enough to hold his interest, and went to investigate bushes around the yard.

Aaron came thundering down the porch stairs in a way that made Shelley flinch, expecting him to fall at any moment. "Bye, Shelley!" he called. "Bye, Dad!" He paused to give Dean a hug, and Shelley stepped back out of his way before she realized he was planning to do the same for her.

"Er…" she knelt uncomfortably and gave Aaron a cautious embrace. It probably looked as weird as it felt, and Shelley was hyper-aware of Deirdre's eyes on her. He smelled like cheese and dirt.

"Do you have my crackers?" he asked, bounding away to put his hand in his mother's. "Bye, Bingo!"

"Right here," Deirdre assured him. "See you on Sunday! Nice to meet you, Shelley!"

It seemed weird to go inside while they were still there, so Shelley stood with Dean and forced herself not to fidget as Aaron buckled himself into a booster seat and Deirdre gave him his crackers, and they finally—finally!—drove away. Aaron waved out the window as Shelley half-heartedly waved after him.

"Well, that was awkward," Dean said cheerfully.

CHAPTER 14

*A*wkward was an understatement, but Dean tried to smile.

Shelley gave him her boardroom smile—the corners of her mouth turned up just exactly the right amount and her face otherwise completely blank. He could feel the roil of confused emotion underlying it, and couldn't blame her.

"So, that was your ex." Her voice was as bland as her face was. "She seems nice."

Bingo, having finished his farewell circle of the lawn, returned to sit next to Shelley and try to lean on her knees adoringly.

Shelley edged back and Bingo leaned further. Shelley took a full step away, and the dog was forced to sit under his own power, choosing instead to lean into space until he flopped over on his side.

"You look beautiful," Dean said, the way he'd originally planned to greet her. And she did look beautiful, like she'd just stepped out of the pages of a fashion magazine. Her legs were long and smooth and her tight skirt barely reached her knees. She was wearing a beige designer jacket against the autumn chill, and a fluttering red scarf that looked too thin to be warm.

Her eyes flickered to his and the smile looked a little more genuine. "Thank you. You look… really great."

Dean might have tried kissing her then, no matter how awkward things seemed, but Bingo was lying between them, and he knew that the moment he stepped over, the dog would stand up, and the opportunity for a kiss would be ruined.

He didn't want her any less than he had in the office of the shop, or when he'd kissed her in front of Gran's Grits. But he wasn't sure how to get from where they were to where they both really wanted to be.

"I made dinner," he said desperately, and the timer had the good grace to go off then.

She followed him into the house, and even if Dean hadn't been able to hear her heels clicking along the floor, he would have known exactly where she was behind him. It wasn't just her smell—how was it possible for someone to *smell* so put-together?—it was the sense of her: a sweet, desperate yearning for her wherever she was.

"I hope you don't mind casserole," he said apologetically. It wasn't city fare, but Dean's sole criteria for the meal was something that could stay in the oven a little longer than intended, or reheat well, in case they got… distracted on the way to the meal.

That hope had been dashed by the chaos that Shelley had come into, and the stiff wall of doubt and discomfort that she'd put up when faced with an unexpected dog and an un-planned-for ex-wife.

"Casserole sounds fine," Shelley said, utterly politely. "Can I help somehow?" She sounded dubious.

"Nothing left to do," Dean assured her. "The table's all set."

"Oh," she said with a smile. "Candles."

They were emergency candles, because that's what Dean could find, but he didn't think they looked too inelegant in the antique holders.

"There's a lighter by the fireplace," he said as he bent to take the casserole from the oven. Damn, he meant to make a fire before she came, something cozy and warm to curl up in front of.

Too late now.

"Get back, Bingo. This isn't for you. Out of the kitchen!"

He heard and felt Shelley go to the fireplace and find the lighter on the mantle.

"This is a cute house," she said quietly, lighting the candles. It was just starting to get dark outside.

"Thanks! I grew up here. Bought it from my parents when they moved to Arizona. Mom couldn't handle the winters, with her asthma." It wasn't as bad as still *living* with his parents, but Dean wondered if it was far off.

"It's a really good use of space," she observed.

Was it code for *this place is tiny and poor*? She did come from a family of millionaires.

He put the casserole on the potholder on the table, and Shelley replaced the lighter on the mantle, nearly tripping over Bingo when she turned around. Bingo wagged his tail and tried to get her to pet him, but Shelley skirted around him carefully.

They sat opposite from each other at the little table and Dean was decidedly weirded out to be looking at his mate —his graceful, gorgeous mate!—in the seat where his son usually sat.

He poured her a glass of wine and they made careful conversation.

She told him that she did contract negotiations for one

of the largest engineering firms in the Midwest and they shared a forced laugh over Shelley's nickname, Shelley the Shark. "I'm not a lawyer like you see in television in court," she explained shyly. "I'm the lawyer that keeps everyone out of court. My specialty is contract law. I help write the contracts and make people sign them, and then use them to make people do what they promised to do."

Dean, feeling rather out-classed, explained that he worked as a mechanic and owned both the shop and the tiny hardware store next door as well.

"Well, the bank owns it, technically, of course. Ted wanted to retire and... well, really no one else wanted it," he said sheepishly. "I scraped the down payment together and it does alright for itself."

"All that and a single dad," Shelley observed. "It probably keeps you really busy."

Dean decided not to add anything about the volunteer work he also did. He'd wanted to fill his life to the seams when Deirdre left him.

"Yeah," he said sheepishly.

"Can I help clear up?" Shelley asked when they were done. "It was delicious."

Dean hadn't made plans for dessert, he realized, standing and letting her help gather her dishes. He should have picked up something from Shaun's bakery.

He'd had high hopes for something else happening after dinner.

Instead, everything was...

"This is weird, isn't it," Shelley said, standing next to him in the kitchen with her plate in one hand and her glass in the other.

"I didn't want it to be weird," he confessed to her. She was so beautiful, and he wanted her so badly that it made it hard to think.

She gave a wry smile that wasn't part of her practiced repertoire and a shy, downcast look. "I thought a mate would be… simple. Straight-forward. Instead…"

"Weird," Dean finished for her.

"Weird," she agreed, putting the dishes on the counter. "Shelley…"

Dean finally accepted his bear's relentless suggestions and stepped forward to kiss her, and then it wasn't weird at all.

CHAPTER 15

*H*is mouth was home, Shelley thought, when he kissed her at last.

Home like she'd never thought a home could be. She longed to be there whenever she wasn't, and it made everything better and safer and sweeter.

He tasted like wine and tater tots, which had never featured in any of the romance books Shelley devoured, but nothing else could have been so perfect.

She kissed him back with all of her heart, winding her arms up around his strong shoulders. As complicated as they had managed to be, this was simple and straightforward. She knew exactly what to do, pulling him as close as they could get while still wearing clothing, passionately kissing him and regretting nothing.

Her lioness growled in her ear, and she knew that his bear was doing the same from the frantic way he was trying to find an enclosure on her shirt and the way he was dragging his teeth along her skin.

She tugged at his shirt, trying to get it off him, trying to pull him... wasn't there a couch in the living room?

Then she gave a shriek as one of her heels hit the threshold for the kitchen and Bingo managed to be directly behind her again. She ungracefully fell over backwards, dragging Dean with her.

"Bingo, out of the kitchen!" Dean said, but it was too late even for shifter reflexes; between her heels and their entanglement, they both went over and Bingo gave a yip of dismay, fled two steps, and then returned to lick everything he could reach.

"Ack, ew, oh my god!" Shelley couldn't help saying, but she was laughing, how could she *not*? There was dog tongue all over her swollen mouth, and in her ear, and across her forehead, and her arms were pinned by Dean's weight so she couldn't squirm very far away. "I'm pretty sure my mascara isn't lick-proof!" she giggled.

Dean was laughing, too, one arm still around her as he shoved the dog with the other. "Bingo, back!" he ordered ineffectively.

They finally regained their feet, chortling and clinging to each other, and Shelley kicked off her heels.

Bingo sat at their feet and looked up, panting hopefully. Clearly he thought he had done something worthy of praise.

"I'm washing my face before I kiss you again," Shelley declared. "My own face," she told Bingo.

As she did, she heard Dean washing his hands in the kitchen sink, scolding Bingo good-naturedly.

She returned from the bathroom in her bare feet.

"You're short," Dean said breathlessly.

"I am not," Shelley protested. He was even more handsome looking flushed from their exertion, and he was smiling more naturally than he had all night. "You just hadn't seen me without heels." She had to look up at him.

"It's hot," Dean said, his grin spreading. How could *teeth* make her knees weak? "Now, where were we?"

"I think we were finding a safer place to continue this," Shelley purred.

"I have a suggestion," Dean said, and he took her by the hand and led her past the disappointed dog and up the stairs, to the bedroom that Shelley had been desperately hoping he was taking her to.

She had shed her shirt before he had a chance to kick the door shut behind them, and was gratified by the way he stopped and stared without breathing at the sight of her blue lace bra.

"Your turn," she told him, pulling up his shirt.

He tore it off so quickly that Shelley heard stitches snap, and then she had her own moment of breathless awe at the vision of his beautiful, broad chest.

She could not have later described how the rest of their clothing came off. She only knew that his fingers were like fire on her skin, and his kisses took her places she'd never imagined. Want and need warred with something deeper, something more real.

Shelley wanted this man differently than she'd ever wanted anyone... or anything... in her entire life.

She wanted to wrap herself around him, protect him, bare herself to him, tell him every secret and learn every one of his. With every piece of clothing, she felt like some part of her shell was peeled away, like he was seeing the real Shelley, not the Shelley she had to show everyone else.

It was only when they were both completely naked that he laid her back on the bed, one hand at her waist, the other catching their fall. His weight on her, his hard cock pressed against her thigh... it was almost too much.

She spread her legs and begged, "Please..."

She was so wet that he slid straight in with just the

slightest change in angle and pressure, and she clawed the bed and rose to meet him.

He paused, buried in her, and Shelley could hear his teeth grind in concentration; he was as tightly wound as she was.

She whimpered and tried to move, craving the friction, and he withdrew a tantalizing inch and drove back in.

A cry escaped her... pleasure and desire... and he thrust again, and again, until they were coupling desperately and Shelley was falling from heights she'd never known.

They lay together a long while afterwards, hands trailing lazily over each other's limbs. He had the most fascinating ripples of muscles, and such long, clever, calloused fingers. Shelley thought she could lie there forever, her whole body utterly content.

Suddenly Dean stiffened in alarm and sat up. "Did anyone blow out the candles?"

"I... I don't think so," Shelley said.

They both scrambled out of bed and raced downstairs naked.

Bingo, who had been sleeping at the foot of the stairs, sprang to his feet in surprise and began barking in random directions, clearly not sure what was happening, but determined to be a part of it.

One of the candles had guttered out entirely and the other was giving its last dying flickers. Hot wax had pooled under the holders.

Dean blew out the remaining flame and Shelley clung to him as they laughed in relief. "I'm sure it would have made a very poor impression to burn down my house on our second date," Dean said sheepishly.

Shelley kissed him. "After what we just did, I would

have forgiven you even having to stand out naked in the cold waiting for the fire department."

To her surprise, Dean blushed. "Considering I'm a third of our fire department, that would be pretty humiliating."

"You're a firefighter?" Shelley exclaimed in surprise.

"Volunteer," Dean said dismissively. "I should have warned you, I'm pretty much always on call. Chances of a call are really slim, our district is just Green Valley and we don't get called out further unless both Farshoot and Dashum are already on multiple jobs; they've got real stations. We're not even NFPA qualified. It's basically some guys with cellphones, ugly suits, and an old surplus Forestry Service truck that I've kept running with duct tape. Most of our callouts are cats in trees and Stanley wanting us to get a tractor out of mud like some kind of free tow service. Why are you staring at me?"

"Because I did not realize that you could get even sexier," Shelley purred, sidling up to him. They were still naked and it seemed like the perfect excuse to touch him.

He leaned over and kissed her, drawing him into her arms where she belonged.

It was like puzzle pieces, or Pringles: everything of her seemed to fit everything of him absolutely perfectly.

"Wait," he murmured. "The curtains are open…"

"Maybe you should close them," Shelley suggested. "For the rest of the weekend…"

"That is a *great* plan," Dean agreed.

CHAPTER 16

*D*ean knew that the closed curtains would have the neighbors talking... but what happened behind them would have caused even more gossip.

They made love on every surface in the house: the kitchen table, the kitchen counter, the washing machine, the couch—which had to be abandoned because Bingo kept sticking cold wet dog nose where it was wildly unwelcome—the stairs, the shower, the sunroom, Dean's desk, the bedroom floor...

Every time that Dean thought they might have finally satisfied their animals' wild needs, Shelley would cast a playful sideways look at him, or he'd accidentally brush up against her, which obviously meant he had to kiss her, and they were off again.

He didn't leave the house except to take Bingo out at odd hours, and they returned swiftly.

He and Shelley didn't really talk in depth until Sunday afternoon, when Deirdre's looming return made them shower in earnest and straighten the house.

"Should I... go?" Shelley asked tentatively, folding the

afghan over the back of the couch. Her face was back in what Dean was calling boardroom mode, perfectly serene if you didn't know her a little.

He knew her more than a little now, didn't he?

Dean stopped scraping wax off the kitchen table and came around to her. "Shelley... I want you to be a part of my life. Of *our* lives. Please stay."

To her credit, she didn't flinch.

"Package deal," she murmured, nodding slowly. "I know."

"But we don't have to do it all at once," Dean reassured her, taking her hands in his own. "We can figure this out as we go. I don't... want it to be awkward."

There was the real smile, the crooked, amused little glimpse of the Shelley beneath the mask.

"We've got a lot of details to resolve," she agreed like the lawyer she was. "Living arrangements, financial decisions... I'd like to read your custody contract."

"My what?"

"Your custody contract. What we do could impact child support or custody schedules."

"I don't even know where the divorce papers are," Dean told her, baffled. "That was five years ago. Deirdre and I just work things out on a week-by-week basis. It changes all the time."

Shelley looked at him skeptically. "You don't have a settlement that says who pays for what or divides your custody time?"

"If Aaron needs something, one of us gets it for him," Dean explained, trying to understand Shelley's surprise. "He's at my house for school because his best friends are here and we try to work out all the weekends and holidays with Deirdre's schedule that we can manage."

Shelley was silent.

Finally, she looked down at her hands where Dean still held them. "I guess I just assumed it was like my parents' divorce, where every hour and dollar was held accountable."

"Deirdre and I don't do that," Dean said gently.

"You still love her."

Dean knew he was quiet too long, but Shelley didn't pull away. "Not like that," he was finally able to say. "Not like *this*."

He looked at the clock. The others wouldn't be there for another half an hour, at least.

"C'mon," he said, pulling her to the couch. "Let me tell you what happened. It's... important that you know." If he didn't tell her, someone else was going to tell her something worse.

Sitting on the couch was an inevitable invitation to Bingo, who immediately jumped up to get cuddles. He could sense the somber mood and didn't attempt to lick anyone or crawl into Shelley's lap. He did sit beside her and lean into her shoulder until she pushed him away and then he lay down and put his head into her lap. After a moment, she stroked his ears and he closed his eyes with a groan of bliss.

Dean wanted to think that her acceptance of Bingo was a good sign of further domestic compatibility, but he knew better than to read too much into it.

"Why isn't Bingo afraid of my lion?" Shelley asked thoughtfully. "Or your bear, for that matter?"

"He's too stupid to fear things," Dean said. "I watched him try to get a big, angry bull to play with him, and you can play fetch with nothing for about an hour before he figures out there never was a ball to start with."

They weren't sitting as comfortably with each other as they had all weekend, draped casually together, but when he put an arm around her, she leaned into him with a sigh.

"Deirdre and I went to high school together. First real love and all, and we thought it would be forever. Forever and a family." Dean paused, waiting for it to be hard to say, and was surprised by how distant it all felt.

"Deirdre's a deer shifter, and we never kept secrets from each other. So… when she met Juan… she came straight to me and she told me."

I'm so sorry, Deirdre had said, weeping. *I didn't ask for this. I never wanted to do this to you.*

"She cheated on you," Shelley said ferociously. Bingo opened his eyes warily. "Maybe I *shouldn't* be here when she gets back."

"No!" Dean said promptly. "I mean, I know that's what people think. It's the obvious answer. But… Juan was her mate. Nothing *happened* until I let her go."

"Oh," Shelley said breathlessly. "*Oh.*"

She returned to petting Bingo and he closed his eyes again, tail thumping on the arm of the couch.

"She offered to stay. For Aaron, and because she'd promised. But I couldn't do that to her. I couldn't keep her, knowing she'd never be happy, just because I wanted her for myself."

Shelley tucked herself closer to Dean's side and he wondered if he only imagined the wave of her love and sympathy.

"I mean, don't think that our marriage was perfect, or that we didn't drive each other crazy on a regular basis. We were two clueless parents in an impossible situation. But Juan loves Aaron as much as Deirdre and I do, and I loved her too much to keep them apart. We had enough reasons to put in the work. Even when it was hard."

He shifted Shelley in his arms and lifted her chin so he

could drown in her eyes. "I didn't understand what Deirdre felt then, I had to trust what she told me. But I understand now, I know how badly that must have torn her up inside, how strong and deep and amazing meeting your mate can be. And I know you don't want all the things I come with, but I know that it's worth it, even if it's hard, and I will do whatever it takes to make *this* work."

CHAPTER 17

*S*helley had spent the weekend thinking there was no possible way to fall harder in love with Dean.

But every time she turned around, there was some new revelation about him: he was a firefighter, he periodically hired a local homeless guy under the table with diner gift certificates, he'd rescued Bingo after he'd been hit by a truck and nursed the tragically dumb mutt back to health. Shelley was beginning to think she must be living in some kind of dream; he was so good, so selfless.

And then he told her how much he loved another woman and managed to make it even *that* about how much he loved *her*.

"Shelley…" he said, in that deep, honey voice. "Shelley, you're crying…"

"I never thought it could be like this," she whispered back. "I never guessed."

Then he was kissing her and Bingo was panting and trying to get in on the action with his tongue, tail wagging against the back of the couch as he squirmed into their laps.

"This… is a lot… harder… with your help…" Dean told the dog between kisses.

Then there was an unexpected beep of a horn from the curb outside and they were drawing away from each other in alarm. Bingo leapt from the couch, barking and running for the door.

Shelley tried to pull herself together, wiping away her tears and straightening her blouse as Dean rose to open the door.

A quick check in her powder mirror showed Shelley that the damage wasn't too bad; she really needed a full round of make-up to feel ready for what was coming, but Dean had convinced her that she shouldn't wear any over the weekend. (It tastes bad! he had complained, and Shelley wasn't willing to risk fewer kisses for flawless matte skin.)

"Why did you honk, Mom?" Aaron was asking as he burst into the house. "You told me that you were only supposed to honk if there was going to be an accident. Was there almost an accident? I didn't see one, was there another car?"

"Never mind, Aaron," Deirdre said cheerfully. "Down, Bingo. Hi, Dean! Hi, Shelley!"

Shelley replied with a tiny *hi* that was completely lost in the chaos that swirled into the house.

Bingo was still barking happily, cavorting around everyone's feet and trying desperately to get someone's attention.

Aaron made a beeline for Dean and was swept up into a tight hug. "Hi Dad!"

Shelley braced herself for another uncomfortable hug, but Aaron, once released, dropped his bag and hat and raced for the kitchen. "I'm starving!"

"Don't believe him if he tells you I didn't feed him this

weekend," Deirdre said, handing Dean what looked like a laundry bag. "He ate two and half hot dogs for lunch and a three-egg omelet this morning for breakfast."

"Growing boy," Dean observed. "Pretty sure I was the same way."

"He's decided he doesn't like bell peppers any more."

"Weren't they his favorite vegetable last week?"

"That was last week. Aaron! I have to go, come give me a hug!"

Aaron trailed out of the kitchen holding an apple with two giant bites out of it.

"Bye, Mom!" he said around the missing part of the apple. He gave her a distracted hug and finally seemed to notice that Shelley was there. "You look less fancy."

Shelley had no idea what to say to that.

"Juan and I want to go out with you two soon—you three," Deirdre corrected herself, ruffling Aaron's hair. "Shelley, we're dying to get to know you, I'm sorry I can't stay, if you're ever in Madison, we've got to have lunch. Dean can give you my number. Dean, give her my number. Bye, sugar! See you next weekend!"

"I thought you had plans next weekend and I had him," Dean said, looking not nearly as bemused as Shelley felt.

"I've rearranged. I'm sure you'll need next weekend off. I'll be on time, promise."

Deirdre winked at Shelley and Shelley felt her cheeks turn scarlet.

There was a flurry of additional 'byes' and hugs and then Deirdre was gone, and it wasn't much quieter without her.

Bingo was still trotting between everyone in the room, tail wagging so enthusiastically it sounded like a drum whenever he passed a wall, and Aaron was talking non-stop about his weekend away. "Mom asked a lot of questions about you," he told Shelley. "We had stuffed peppers for dinner but I didn't eat the pepper part but the middle was really good. It had sausage and cheese."

"Oh," Shelley managed before he was going on.

"Mom didn't let me watch *Iron Man*, can we watch *Iron Man*? Trevor's seen *Iron Man* and I really really really really really want to see it."

"We were just talking about what we were going to do tonight," Dean said peaceably. "What were you thinking about, Shelley?"

Shelley looked gravely down at Aaron. He had hazel eyes just like Dean, but she could see some of Deirdre's face shape beneath his childish cheeks, and he had her curly hair. "I thought I would stay for dinner and sleep here tonight and... tomorrow I might go to Minneapolis and spend a day or two getting a few of my things to bring over and extending my leave of absence at work. I'd stay here for a while, if that's okay."

"Can we watch a movie?" Aaron asked, clearly not caring about the rest of the plan.

Dean was not looking at Aaron, he was looking at Shelley and his eyes were like suns. "Sure, kiddo. Anything you want."

"Can we watch *Deadpool*?" Aaron tested.

"Goodness, no!" Shelley surprised herself by saying at the same time as Dean said, "No!" Even she knew *that* much.

Aaron shrugged and grinned.

"I'll go start dinner," Dean said. Shelley wondered if she'd been wrong about seeing Deirdre in the little boy's face, because their grins were exactly the same. "Who wants grilled cheese on the couch while we watch *Iron Man*?"

"Meeeeeeee!" Aaron hollered.

"Yes, please!" Shelley said with a smile. "I'll get the movie set up."

Aaron, still chewing on his apple, directed her, showing her which remote was which. Shelley reminded herself that his sticky fingers wouldn't do any lasting damage.

As they settled onto the couch with plates of grilled cheese and carrot sticks, Shelley found herself wondering if being there *really* was all that she needed to do.

Because she was sure there wasn't anywhere else she would rather be.

She fed Bingo her carrots.

CHAPTER 18

*D*ean hadn't known that he could miss someone after knowing them such a short, precious time.

The days without Shelley felt endless.

They talked together every night on the phone like teenagers, about every subject under the sun except the ones that mattered, and neither of them wanted to be the first to hang up.

He texted her a photo of Aaron's first lost tooth before he thought to text it to Deirdre, then wondered if he should done it as a group text, then despaired at the complexities of the situation.

Shelley texted him back a photo of her Inbox, piled high with contracts, and despaired of ever making it back. "Thursday, I hope."

Sexting turned out as awkward as their second date, without the kiss to take it from weird to wonderful.

He did a brake pad replacement on Mrs. Fredrickson's beater... and gapped the spark plugs and topped off the oil while he had it in, neither telling her, nor charging her. He sold a new outdoor spigot to Old George, and a basket of plumbing parts to a rather frigid Gillian. Stanley spent an hour in his store telling him about all the ways that things used to be constructed better, then bought one thirty-three cent carpenter's pencil with exact change.

Dean got a call-out halfway through the week and got into full turnout gear for the report of a fire.

When he and Turner arrived, it turned out to be a backyard brush pile fire being carefully watched by a man who could produce a county burn license and had a garden hose coiled nearby.

The neighbor who had called it in was not remorseful. "Could have burned down the whole town!" she said with a sniff. "And it took you long enough to get here. Your new girlfriend keeping you too busy to be a hero anymore?"

News of his weekend with Shelley had spread like the fire the neighbor predicted.

When Dean walked into Gran's Grits that night, the waitress smirked at him.

"Over here!"

Andrea was sitting with Shaun and Trevor at the big curved booth in the corner. Aaron bolted to sit next to Trevor and argue over the best crayons.

Their most recent feud seemed to be over, at least.

Aaron had been telling all his friends at school, rather prematurely perhaps, that Trevor's aunt was going to come live with them and that made them basically cousins. They then made Clara cry by pointing out that she didn't have any cousins, felt bad about her tears, and got in a fight with each other.

Andrea had orchestrated this dinner with the pretense of making sure the boys mended fences.

But she was clearly not there for a long-forgotten argument and her smile was predatory.

"Sorry," Shaun said with a shrug as Dean took his seat

beside Aaron. "She's been grilling me all week and I told her that if she wanted to know anything else, she'd have to ask you."

"Thanks," Dean said wryly. He gave a resigned sigh. "What do you want to know, Andrea?"

Andrea, apparently, wanted to know everything. When was Shelley returning? Were they going to be living together? Looking for a new house? Getting married? Had she met Deirdre? Did she get along with Bingo?

Dean only realized halfway through that he was grinning helplessly during her entire interrogation.

Shaun seemed mostly mystified by the new development, if grudgingly accepting.

"I dunno," he said skeptically. "I'm suspecting body-snatchers, because nothing you have said even resembles my sister. My sister does not like dogs. My sister does not like kids. My sister likes clothes and make-up and making grown men cry over clauses and terms. Do you know they call her Shelley the Shark in some circles?"

Trevor found that hilarious and repeated 'Aunt Shelley the Shark!' several times until Andrea shook her head at him disapprovingly.

Aaron looked suspiciously at Shaun and didn't say anything.

Walking home together after dinner, Aaron was unexpectedly clingy, and wanted to hold Dean's hand. It seemed tiny and fragile in his.

Aaron didn't say much during the usual slow progression through the chores of going to bed, but after Dean had tucked him in, read a chapter of their current book, and turned off the light, a small voice called him back.

"Dad?"

Dean paused in the hallway and looked back through the doorway. "Yeah?"

"Does Shelley like me?"

Dean froze, then quickly lied, "Yeah, of course." *Was* it a lie? Was Aaron something she had to endure on his behalf, or was she actually warming up to him?

"Trevor's dad said she doesn't like kids."

"She's just… not used to kids. That doesn't mean she doesn't like you."

Aaron digested that in silence.

"Will I have to go away and live with Mom and Juan all the time?" he asked plaintively.

Dean was back in the room in a flash, kneeling by the bed. "Never," he promised. "I would never do that."

Aaron sat up, face serious in the light of multicolored nightlights. "But if she doesn't like me…"

"Do you remember when we got Bingo?" Dean asked.

"Yeaaaahhhh?" Aaron said in tones that didn't indicate he actually did.

"You were afraid that because I had Bingo to love that I wouldn't love you anymore."

"Yeeeeaaaaaahhhh."

"Did that happen?"

"Nooooooo."

"No matter who else there is, no matter what else happens, you and me, we're a team. That doesn't mean that you and I won't be in other teams, like your mom and Juan are a team, and you and Trevor are a team, and maybe me and Shelley will be a team. But you and me… you and me will always be a team, too."

That seemed to satisfy Aaron. He snuggled back into his pile of blankets and seventy stuffed animals and Dean tucked a few more around him. By morning they would be scattered on the floor and Aaron would be sleeping soundly, sideways in the bed.

The second call-out that week was the next day: an old

farmer who'd taken a fall and undoubtedly broken his ankle. It was faster to send Turner with the fire truck to take him to the first care in the next town over for x-rays and a brace than it was to wait for an ambulance, so Dean walked back to the shop in half his turnout gear.

Someone had made a purchase and left cash on the counter. He had no idea what had been bought or who had bought it. Hopefully it would come out even at inventory time.

It was the third call-out that upended his life.

CHAPTER 19

Shelley half-heartedly scrolled through her Instagram feed as she waited for the elevator, liking occasional random posts, then went through the messages she'd been ignoring.

"What are you wearing, girlfriend? Missing your photos on IG! <3"

"Let's do lunch and snark about the Sallies fashion show!"

"Shell! I need you to alter a dress for a date TONIGHT. Drinks on me!" (It was from nearly a week ago)

"Check out my new boots! OMG! They cost $500 but my feet deserve it!"

Had she never recognized how shallow and substanceless her life really was? In trying to pack, she realized she had a wardrobe of clothing she'd only worn once, and nothing was practical. It was a sea of silk and fine Egyptian cotton and the best Shetland wool, the finest vegan leather, all name brands or handcrafted.

But she had nothing the slightest bit suitable to wear for walking a dog in the woods, or playing ball with a seven-year-old.

Did moms even play ball? Was that just a dad thing? Were gender roles still in place like that?

Pinterest assured her that moms and their sons did precious crafts together with old buttons and lace scraps, and baked healthy cookies, while wearing cute pastel plaid shirts and jeans.

"Are you really quitting? Didn't we just lose your father?"

Shelley looked up to find that Jack, co-owner of the company, had joined her in the wait for the elevator.

She hadn't intended to quit, only to extend her leave of absence for a week or two, go back and make sure this thing with Dean was really a thing… and then convince him to come live with her here.

But this wasn't a life for him, and it certainly wasn't a life for Aaron. She'd never noticed how distant people here were, compared to Green Valley. She knew the names of the pets at her condo, but not their human owners. She locked and dead bolted her condo door and remembered that Dean never even locked his shop.

And she knew beyond the shadow of a doubt that she didn't belong here without him.

"I'm trying to get the Connor contract finished before I go," she promised. "And you can always call me if you have questions."

"This isn't two weeks' notice," Jack said, frowning.

"I'm spending two weeks' vacation time," Shelley said icily. "Would you like to argue about the details of my employment contract?"

Jack laughed. "I wouldn't dare," he said peacefully. "I'm sorry to hear you're going, and I hope you will be available for consulting work in the future."

Shelley nodded. "You have my contact information; I'm very amenable to helping you in the future. As my schedule allows."

Jack looked at her with curiosity that he was doing a poor job of hiding. "What is it you're going to be doing in Green Valley...?"

Shelley stared back at him.

She was going to be a *mom*.

Because her mate was a package deal, and she already couldn't imagine her life without him.

It was ridiculous, and she'd known this guy a few days, and kids terrified her, and here she was, quitting her job and weeding through her impractical shoes and wondering where she could buy hiking boots that didn't make her look like an elephant.

Shelley realized she was still staring at Jack without answering, with her very best blank expression plastered over her face, and he was starting to squirm like he was being interrogated. "Sorry to pry," he said sheepishly as the elevator reached their floor.

Shelley blinked. "No, no, it's fine. It's... just... an unexpected life change."

"Not a bad one, I hope," Jack said sincerely. "You and your dad are okay?"

Shelley walked into the elevator next to him and smiled at her own reflection as Jack pressed the lobby button. "Yeah," she said in wonder. "More than okay. It's really good." *I got this.*

We got this, her lioness reminded her.

She left Jack utterly mystified behind her as she walked

swiftly to the parking garage, her heels clicking across the concrete.

CHAPTER 20

Dean was just biting into a sandwich at his dining room table when the call came. He put it down reluctantly and shoved his phone in his pocket.

His house was only a block and a half from the station, so he planned to simply jog there, but what he saw when he got to the sidewalk and had a view down the street froze his feet to the ground.

Oily black smoke was pouring from his shop down the street, dark and ominous against the sunny day.

Dean made his feet move at last, bolting down the block.

A small, alarmed crowd was starting to gather, pointing and talking.

Black, acrid smoke pouring from around the garage door, turning the familiar lines of his shop and the store next door into wavery alien shapes. It was eerie, and so quiet that Dean could hear the crackle of flames from within, even though he couldn't see any yet.

Dean had to make the split-second decision: sprint two

buildings down to the station and get into turnout gear, or battle the blaze *now* in the clothes he was wearing.

Seconds mattered in structure fires. Dean did a conscious check for loose clothing, tucked his pants awkwardly into his boots (he was, at least, wearing fire-boots), pulled a handkerchief from a pocket to tie around his face, and waded in to assess.

The office door handle wasn't hot, but the office was thick with dark smoke that burned at Dean's throat. This wasn't friendly campfire smoke, to make eyes water and send people scrambling for new seats when the wind shifted; this was its demon cousin, sending harsh fingers of pain instantly to protesting lungs.

There was no fire here, yet, but the smoke was coming in all around the door to the shop. Dean ducked impulsively into the bathroom, turned on the tap, and then broke off the faucet so that the water was squirting directly into the air, soaking the entire bathroom. He didn't have a sprinkler system, but he could improvise, and the bathroom was nestled between the shop and the store. If he couldn't save one, maybe he could save the other. He wet his handkerchief, and for good measure, got as much of himself wet as he could.

The fuse box was between the bathroom and the door to the store, and Dean wrenched the door to it open and shut off every fuse in succession. Something sparked, there was a crash from the garage, and the dim light on the coffee maker went out. It would be better to kill the main breaker, but that was around back, and at least another few minutes of detour. This would at least keep outlets from being active and prevent live wires.

There was an industrial-sized fire extinguisher behind the counter, and Dean could only find it by feel, grasping around and coughing. It was a comfortable heft in his hands, and he drew in a breath that hurt to the bottom of his stomach, knowing it would be the best breath he would have until this was over.

Then he kicked in the door to the shop, not even bothering to try the handle, and the heat and smoke doubled in intensity.

He couldn't see flames—the oily smoke was too thick—but he could see dirty flickering light, and hear the roar of the fire. It must be towards the back of the shop, to his right, against the wall to the bathroom. There was another extinguisher inside the door, so Dean wasn't frugal with the one he was holding, knocking off the safety and spraying everything in the direction of worst heat.

He held a map of the shop in his head, trying to figure out what was on fire, what hazards he wouldn't be able to see; it would be deadly to trip over the lift, or knock over an oil can. The welding setup was fortunately on the other side of the garage near the overhead door; the oxy-acetylene tanks were as far from the inferno as possible.

His eyes watered uncontrollably; even if the shop had not been filled with impenetrable smoke, he would have been blind.

I can smell, his bear told him helpfully. *The fire is* there.

Dean forged forward, hopeful he wasn't letting any fire get behind him, and he could hear when he managed to hit open flame by the angry hiss of dying fire. He unloaded the extinguisher in that area, completely blind by now, choking for air, and trusting his bear's direction.

It grew gradually lighter in his hands, and Dean finally threw away the empty cylinder. Another extinguisher. He had another. It was back by the door to the office, an agonizing distance behind him, now. Somewhere, glass shattered.

Dean turned, and had no idea which direction to go.

He could hear the fire, which had begun to gutter under his assault, gain new strength.

Behind him.

Never let the fire get behind you.

Dean was down on his knees now, pressing the hand-kerchief to his mouth and dragging air through it. Should he shift? Would it do any good, or just confuse a coroner later?

Then he heard the wail of a siren, an uncommon sound in the sleepy little town of Green Valley, and there was a sudden rush of fresh air to his lungs as the overhead door was wrenched open with a grinding squeal.

"Dean, you moron!"

"Get the water on!"

"Do you see him?"

"Don't hit him with the spray!"

Then Dean heard the grumbling motor of the water cannon pump, and the roar of water.

"Let's go, you idiot." Someone in turnout gear, voice muffled by their SBCA, had an arm under him, helping him back up. Carter, Dean realized.

Turner must be on the water cannon, which was blasting into the garage to one side of him, creating waves of thick steam that mixed with the smoke, hot and thick.

Dean tried to get his feet under him, failed, and when he tried to breathe there was only fire and darkness.

CHAPTER 21

*S*helley didn't realize exactly how many people lived in Green Valley until she drove in that afternoon and found the entire population gathered downtown. For a moment, she thought there was some kind of celebration going on—then she recognized the flashing lights as a police car, and an ambulance—and they were right in front of Dean's shop.

But it wasn't Dean's shop, it was a ruin of Dean's shop, blackened and burnt, and the side of the store was coated in soot.

There were too many people for Shelley to pull directly up to the action, so she parked the car at the nearest curb and jumped out.

"Dean, Dean?"

Shelley pushed her way carelessly through the crowd and found him at last, sitting on the sidewalk with his head in his hands. He was almost black with soot, and his shoulders were slumped in exhaustion and defeat. He was flapping a hand at an EMT who was trying to put a blood pressure cuff on him.

Seeing him did a whole host of things to Shelley's insides. She was terrified and joyful and relieved and she wanted him even though he was as dirty as she'd ever seen anyone in her life. She hardly even noticed the people who were staring and whispering and standing around gossiping about the fire.

"Dean," Shelley said in soft sympathy as she sat down beside him. "Dean, your shop, I'm so sorry. Are you okay?"

He gave her a desperate look, longing and hungry, then his expression shuttered in a way that Shelley practiced in the mirror.

"No one was hurt," he said roughly. "That's the important part. No one got hurt."

The grief in his voice belied his optimistic words.

Shelley had seen the damage to the building; she knew that the shop was a total loss, and it was something of a miracle that the attached hardware store wasn't also.

She tried to put an arm around him, but Dean stopped her. "You'll ruin your jacket."

"I don't care," Shelley said honestly. "It's just a jacket." But she settled for taking Dean's ash-blackened hand. He held onto her hand like he was drowning and Shelley's world reduced to his touch. This was not the reunion she had imagined. The kisses she'd fantasized seemed impossible in these circumstances.

She was keenly aware of her out-of-place businesswear and the eyes of the grandmas and gawkers. A few people were taking pictures on their phones.

"You're an idiot, Dean."

Shelley looked up with a flash of anger, to see a fire-fighter nearly as dirty as Dean standing behind them.

"I'm glad you got there when you did, Turner," Dean said simply, without looking back.

"What the hell were you thinking, Dean? You don't go

into structure fires without gear."

"Saved the shop," Dean said grimly. "Maybe more."

"It wasn't worth the risk!" Turner said sharply. He was older than Dean, with a head of silvered brown hair. His glance at Shelley was unfriendly.

Shelley's hand tightened in Dean's. She wasn't sure which one of them was squeezing.

"I thought it was," Dean protested, standing and turning stiffly to face him, dropping Shelley's hand as he did. Shelley got to her feet and barely kept herself from trying to get between them to protect Dean. She had to fight to rein in her lioness' instincts. This wasn't her battle, even if it was her mate.

"I disagree," Turner growled. "You're reckless and irresponsible, and this isn't the first time you've made a stupid choice."

Dean's hands went into fists at his side. "No one got hurt."

"You'd be dead if I hadn't gotten here when I did," Turner reminded him.

Dean didn't deny it.

"Look, Dean, I'm not going to watch you break your kid's heart. You're off the squad."

"You can't do that," Dean said in disbelief. The catch of his breath made him cough alarmingly and Shelley swayed in place keeping herself from reaching out to him.

"I just did," Turner said gruffly.

"There are only three of us," Dean reminded him hoarsely.

"Now there's two."

Shelley wanted to step in, wanted to do... anything. But she knew that she was an outsider here, an unknown stranger, so she hovered anxiously to one side and steamed.

"Look," Turner said more gently. "You've got a big

mess here to deal with, and a kid, and—" he glanced at Shelley skeptically but didn't finish the sentence. "Maybe you just need a little time off. I'm not saying this is permanent, I'm just saying you need a break. Because stupid—"

"It wasn't stupid," Dean growled.

"*Stupid* decisions are going to do more harm than good."

"You're making a mistake," Dean told him, shaking his head.

"It's mine to make," Turner said firmly.

Someone called from within the burnt-out garage, "Hey, Turner!" and he left Dean with a final scowl and one sour glance at Shelley.

"Dean…" she said achingly.

He shrugged, angry and distant. Shelley could feel the prickles of humiliation and despair from him.

"Can I help?" she asked desperately. "If you need money to rebuild…"

"I don't want your money!"

Shelley had never heard Dean angry. She knew that he was hurting, and feeling uncertain; it was like a wave of emotions that wasn't hers, and she knew just as clearly that his anger wasn't intended for her, but for himself.

"It doesn't have to be money," she said gently. "If there's something else I can do…"

He gave a great, tired sigh. "Aaron gets off from school in an hour. I've… got a lot of paperwork and cleanup to do. Could you see that he does his homework, and get him dinner? I… might be home really late."

Babysit.

He wanted her to babysit.

Without a single hesitation, Shelley said, "Yes. I can do that."

Even as she wondered if she really *could*.

CHAPTER 22

*D*ean knew what kind of courage it took Shelley to accept his request to watch Aaron; even through his anger and frustration he could feel her fear and resolve.

"Thanks," he growled. "The house is unlocked. You can ask at the neighbors if you need anything."

"We'll manage fine," Shelley said serenely from behind her smile.

He considered kissing her, because it had been four whole days since he'd last tasted her lips, but the murmurs of the gawkers and the prying eyes of the gathered neighbors made him hesitate.

She was the one who stepped forward and gave him a perfectly chaste kiss on his sooty cheek, then walked away down the sidewalk with her heels clicking.

Dean felt like his world was walking away and wished he could call her back. He wanted her arms around him, he wanted the smell of her to chase away the reek of smoke in his nose.

He wanted his chest to stop hurting.

I can help you, his bear promised. *We'll find a quiet place and I can help heal you.*

Dean reached for the phone that had been in his pocket, but it refused to turn on. He wasn't sure if it had gotten too hot, if he'd fallen on it, or if smoke had somehow damaged it. Maybe the battery was just dead.

He felt made of smoke, like it had crept into all his pores and transformed him into something dark and oily.

And Turner... maybe Turner wasn't wrong.

"Are you Dean James?"

Dean looked up from his contemplation of his dead phone to find a paunchy, frowning man regarding him.

"I'm Dean," he offered cautiously. It was unusual to see strangers in Green Valley.

"Fred Averly," the man said, offering a hand. "I'm the adjuster with Midwest Insurance."

Dean shook Fred's hand. He'd bought the policy on-line when he first bought the shop and attached store. He held up his phone. "I haven't even had a chance to call them yet."

Fred's smile looked forced. "I've already talked to the police and requested a copy of the incident report, but I understand that you were the first one on the scene." His look was nothing short of suspicious.

"Yes," Dean said, as mildly as he could. Was he going to be accused of insurance fraud? His bear growled a warning from his chest. "I'm... I *was* part of the volunteer fire department." Did that seem too pat?

Fred looked him up and down even more skeptically, then started handing Dean paperwork. "It's best if you get these things filled out as quickly as possible so we can expedite your claim. Do you mind if I start taking photographs?"

Dean took the forms, leaving dirty fingerprints on

every page as he flipped through them. "Go ahead. The cops already have some."

The shop had stopped smoldering, and Fred fastidiously went into what was left of it, careful not to brush up against anything in his cheap suit as he started snapping shots.

Dean watched him a little while, then took the forms and walked to the fire station for a shower; he had a set of spare clothes there, and what he was wearing couldn't be salvaged. Maybe Carter could help him figure out the forms when he'd gotten the worst of the black off.

But it wasn't Carter who was sitting at the crew table when Dean staggered out of the shower, it was Turner.

The station was little more than a glorified garage, with a basic bathroom in the back, a work bench and a table with three chairs that was comfortable to sit at only if the fire truck—a battered surplus wildfire truck—wasn't parked there occupying most of the space.

Dean had left the paperwork sitting on the table, and Turner was flipping through it thoughtfully.

"Pretty ridiculous how much crap they think people keep track of," he said dismissively. "Who the hell knows when the last time the trees were cleared back from the edge of the building."

"Probably when the place was built in sixty-three," Dean suggested warily. He still sounded like a lifetime smoker, his voice rough. If he breathed too deep, he coughed.

There was coffee in the pot and Dean took a cup, black, and sat down across from Turner, mostly because his legs didn't want to hold him up anymore. His bear was anxious to get somewhere to shift, but Dean wasn't even sure if he could get somewhere private without collapsing.

The hot shower had taken more out of him than he expected.

"I wasn't kidding," Turner said, putting the paperwork down.

"Maybe they figure the claim period will expire before I can get everything filled out," Dean said with a crooked grin. The coffee was old, but still hot.

"I'm not talking about the insurance crap," Turner said grimly.

"I'm not sorry," Dean grumbled. "It turned out fine."

"I'm not even really talking about this fire," Turner said, taking off his hat and rubbing his short hair. "Dean, you've been... really hard on yourself since... since Deirdre left you."

Dean blinked at him. He hadn't thought about Deirdre once that day. He wondered if anyone had called and told her about the fire yet. The town had pretty well turned against her during their divorce, despite his best efforts, but gossip was gossip and it would be hard for some of the town hens to resist sharing the news.

"You've been taking a lot of unnecessary risks," Turner pointed out. "Not just on call-outs, either. You've pretty well bankrupted yourself on that shop, haven't you? Is that why you went in to try to save it?"

Dean scowled across the table, the coffee cup clenched in his hands. He didn't answer.

"Look, Dean, you've got friends, people who care about you..."

"If you remind me about Aaron and give me a guilt trip about taking risks when I've got a kid at home..."

Turner frowned. "That's not where I'm going with this. You've been burning your candle at both ends, Dean. That's not good for you, and no, that's not good for Aaron, and it's not good for your judgment. What I'm saying is that you should just step back a little, take a break. Regroup. That girl…"

Shelley. His mate. "What about her?" He sounded as defensive as he felt.

"You serious about her?" Turner's look across the table was suspicious.

Serious didn't begin to cover what he felt for Shelley. He was more serious than he'd ever been in his life, more determined, more focused. "Yeah. Yeah, I am."

"I wouldn't have guessed she was your type, but she's a fine-looking woman, and you look happy with her. So go do that, for you."

"What do you mean…?"

"You've been doing what's right for everyone else, Dean. Ever since you got out of high school, you were working for other people, arranging your life trying to be everything to everyone. You can't be the best business owner and the best mechanic and the best dad and the best fire fighter all at once. Take a step back, try to be the best for you for once."

"Is that why you pulled me off the squad?" Dean protested. "Because you're trying to play psychiatrist? Green Valley needs…"

Turner stopped him. "Jamie's coming back from her summer job in Alaska next week, we'll put her on the squad for the winter. We can re-evaluate your participation in the spring. See where the store is, what the shop is doing… where you are with your new girl. Green Valley Fire can weather a season without you."

Dean knew when he was beaten, and to be honest, felt a little relieved.

If he had to admit it, he was tired. Not just the bone-deep tired from inhaling too much smoke and standing in the hot shower too long. It was the tired of working two jobs on top of being a small town firefighter and trying to be an on-point single dad. It was the exhausted tired of keeping a brave face to the world, pretending he didn't feel completely alone.

And now there was Shelley, and he didn't have to be alone. Suddenly, the heart-whole face he tried to show to the world was the unexpected truth, and everything else felt like empty busyness.

Turner, watching him, must have guessed at the turmoil in Dean's chest. "If you need a reference, I'll vouch for you." He put a hand across the table and Dean thoughtfully shook it.

CHAPTER 23

Shelley stood in the middle of the house and stared around. Bingo sat down and leaned against her while she absently scratched his ears. His tail beat a steady swishing thump on the floor.

She wasn't ready for this, for Aaron without Dean to act as a buffer. There was no way she could handle an active seven-year-old boy by *herself*.

There weren't enough mom blogs in the world to prepare her.

Shelley could feel the panic rising in her throat. She'd kept it under control with Dean, because Dean needed her, and because she was an expert at keeping everything stuffed down around other people.

Except that Dean *didn't* need her.

He didn't want her money, he knew she was hopeless at… at basically everything useful. She didn't know what to do with dogs or kids, she couldn't cook, and she was barely capable of cleaning. She had brought her car to the shop with a *loose license plate*.

Dean hadn't asked her to quit her job; he probably knew that this whole thing was doomed. She'd just been impulsive and stupid and overly-optimistic and she'd felt like maybe a mate could fix her, and here she was on the brink of a panic attack because she was pretty sure she couldn't do the *one thing* he'd asked of her…

Her hand was wet.

Bingo was licking her hand enthusiastically, because she'd stopped scratching his ears.

Shelley crouched tentatively. "You're a good dog," she said, because that seemed to be what you were supposed to say to a dog.

Bingo obviously thought this was the best thing anyone had *ever* said to him, and went into a spasm of wiggling and wagging his tail and butting his head against Shelley's neck and licking the air noisily. Only shifter strength kept Shelley from keeling over backwards at his loving assault.

"Okay, that's good, that's enough, down or back, or whatever," Shelley said, but she laughed as she said it, and scratched his ears.

Suddenly Bingo's ears pricked and he gave a happy bark and bounded for the door, just as Aaron threw it open. "Dad?"

Bingo gave him a joyous lick and bounced around him, sniffing his backpack hopefully.

"Hi Aaron," Shelley said, standing up again.

Aaron's face understandably fell. "Oh, hi." He dropped his backpack in a heap by the door and Bingo investigated it with a wagging tail.

"Your dad is really busy tonight getting everything sorted at the auto shop," Shelley explained nervously. "He asked me to come over and keep an eye on you."

Aaron shrugged. "Okay," he said morosely. He

wandered towards the kitchen and Shelley followed him helplessly.

He must be worried about his dad, about his dad's shop. Shelley resisted the urge to use her smart phone to look up 'cheering up 7-yr-old.'

"Do you, ah… want a snack?" Hadn't he been all about eating the last few times she'd seen him?

"Maybe."

Bingo gave up on his search of the backpack to trot into the kitchen hopefully and Aaron hugged him around the neck and ruffled his ears.

"Do you want something to drink?" Shelley tried desperately. What else did kids *do*?

"Nah," Aaron repeated.

Shelley had already opened the fridge and was frowning into it. There was some kind of meat, thawing in a shallow dish, a few dubious leftovers in tupperware that Shelley couldn't identify, as well as vegetables, milk, eggs, cheese. Not food, just ingredients. "Carrots?" Shelley offered helplessly.

Aaron flopped down on the floor with Bingo and they started roughhousing, Bingo licking and wagging his tail so vigorously that his entire backend was in motion. They hit the little table in the corner and it danced in place.

Shelley shut the fridge door and stared at them in consternation. Was this the kind of activity she should discourage? Or would that just make her a big meanie? She thought longingly of the pills in her purse, but they left her feeling wrung out and slightly dazed. She needed all of her wits for this large challenge in a small package.

She was saved having to make any decisions by a knock on the door.

Bingo went into a flurry of happy barks, bounding for

the front of the house. Shelley kneed him out of the way and opened the door to a woman with gray braids that she recognized from her father's wedding; one of Tawny's friends. She was holding a casserole dish and Shelley hoped they hadn't been introduced before because she had no idea what her name was.

She looked at Shelley without smiling. "Brought a casserole for Dean," she said.

"Oh," Shelley said, equally surprised. That was a thing people actually did? "Thank you..." she was trying to keep Bingo back, hampered by Aaron trying to squeeze around her other side to see what was happening.

"Who is it?"

"Shame about his shop," the woman said. "Very tragic."

"Yes," Shelley agreed. "Very trag... oh, Bingo!"

The dog escaped and trotted straight to the woman, who was not very tall. She put the casserole up in the air, which Bingo took as a challenge, bouncing to investigate.

"Bingo, no! Sit! Don't!" Shelley cried, as Aaron came around her other side saying, "Hi Mrs. Fredrickson!"

Shelley took Bingo by the scruff of the neck and held him firmly back, only wondering afterwards if it was a demonstration of more strength than she ought to show. "I'm so sorry," she said, trying to make it look as if she was struggling. "Sit!"

Bingo panted happily and sat, tail swishing on the porch. Shelley tentatively let go of him and he flopped over on his side, pretending he'd never had any interest in the casserole whatsoever.

"I'm Marta," the woman introduced herself. "Marta Fredrickson. I live in the brick house on Parker."

"Shelley," she said, feeling shy. "Shelley Powell."

Marta gave her a narrow-eyed look. "You're Shaun's sister, then. Damien's daughter."

"I... yes."

"Lot of you Powells around these days with your money and your shiny cars," Marta said with a sniff. She handed the casserole to Shelley. "Heat it up for 30 minutes at 350." She said it dubiously, as if Shelley might not be capable of such a task.

"Thank you," Shelley said, blinking at her. "It's very... er... kind of you."

Marta made a harrumph, and Shelley couldn't decide what she meant by it. "Dean's a good young man," the woman said, and her skeptical look at Shelley's impractical heels said plenty.

Aaron had disappeared, and Shelley wished she could do the same. Bingo had sat up to lick himself noisily, one leg in the air as he investigated his genitals with his tongue.

Trying not to laugh at the absurdity, Shelley politely agreed, "Dean *is* a good man. He will appreciate the casserole very much and I will tell him that you stopped by. Thank you."

Marta seemed pleased by her response and nodded crisply. "You'll do," she said cryptically, with a glance at Bingo, who was still very busily grooming himself. "Good luck."

Shelley closed the door behind her, mystified, and brought the casserole dish in to the kitchen.

"I don't want to eat that," Aaron declared.

Shelley supposed she should be glad that he had waited until Marta had left to voice his opinion.

She didn't particularly want to eat it, either, but knew she should say something to set a good example. "It was very kind of Mrs. Fredrickson to bring it by." She sounded unbelievably uptight.

ZOE CHANT

The casserole looked singularly unappealing, with its hard brown noodles and green peas. Canned peas, Shelley suspected. It definitely didn't look anywhere near the caliber of the casserole Dean had made her. "Maybe it tastes better than it looks?"

It didn't.

Shelley sat across from Aaron at the table and they both pushed it around on their plates and took skeptical bites that weren't rewarded.

"Oh, screw it," Shelley finally said, causing Aaron's head to jerk up and his eyes to go wide. Shelley put down her fork and stood up. "Get your jacket, Aaron. We're going shopping." She put on her jacket and sunglasses and swung her purse over a shoulder.

Aaron obediently grabbed his jacket and stuffed his arms into it, never once taking his eyes off of her. "What are we shopping for?" he asked.

"Junk food."

Aaron nearly fell over Bingo, who had gotten excited by people putting on coats and was trying to make sure no one forgot him.

"Junk food?" Aaron shoved Bingo back from the door as Shelley opened it.

"Junk food," Shelley said firmly. "There are some days that require it, and this is obviously one of them."

Bingo whined as they shut the door and shortly appeared in the window, looking wistfully after them.

It took a little effort to figure out how to walk with the little boy; Shelley was used to a long, confident stride, but he had to scamper to keep up, and then when she tried to take shorter steps, he was pulling her faster.

The grocery store had no name out front, but Shelley was sure it must be named Shirley's or Mary's or Mom's.

Shelley took a basket at the door. Aaron, his hand still in hers, led her directly to an aisle of treasures.

"What do you want to get?" Shelley asked, snagging a personal bag of ridged potato chips for herself.

Aaron start to agonize between cheese puffs and seasoned corn chips. Shelley waited for a few moments as he hemmed and hawed, then tipped both of them into her basket. "We're going to need chocolate," she declared.

Sweets were on the next aisle over, beside a display of rakes and cow-patterned garden gloves. Hot tamales went into the basket, and a bag of peanut M&Ms. "They have nuts in them, so they're sort of healthy," Shelley told Aaron. "Next we'll need root beer."

Aaron looked at her like she'd just announced that down was up and led her to the tiny soda display, where Shelley grabbed a liter of root beer. "Ice cream," she directed Aaron, whose eyes got very big indeed.

There were two upright freezer displays and one small chest freezer, absolutely jam-packed with local meat, frozen vegetables, and an eclectic selection of expired ice cream. Shelley selected a pint of vanilla almost unreadable with frost.

"They have corn dogs," Aaron said wistfully, and Shelley remembered how avidly he'd eaten them at Gran's Grits.

Shelley picked up the box of frozen corn dogs and threw them into her heaping basket as well. "Where do we check out?"

The vacant cashier's desk was cluttered with stands selling candy, and obviously home-printed pamphlets for local churches. There was a t-shirt rack sporting cheap Halloween costumes in all sizes.

"Have you thought about what you want to be for

Halloween?" Shelley asked as they waited for someone to show up.

"I want to be the Flash!" Aaron said enthusiastically, flipping through the offerings. There were seven sizes of ice queen costumes, an Iron Man, a few Batmen, a scarecrow, two pirates, and several sexy nurses and police officers in adult sizes.

Shelley fingered the cheap material and the terrible seams and frowned. "Do you want me to make you a costume?" Halloween was a few weeks out; it shouldn't be too hard to whip up a pair of pajamas in the right color and applique a logo.

Aaron was staring at her. "You can *do* that?"

Was it a dig on her ability to do anything?

"Sure, I sew all kinds of things," Shelley said. It would be a first for a kid's costume, but Shelley wasn't going to mention that. She altered her own clothing all the time, and she'd made a lot of doll clothing as a child, this would just be halfway in between. She eyed the cluttered store. "Do they sell fabric here?"

The fabric section was next to some dusty greeting cards. It was one shelf about three feet wide, and nearly half of the selection was plaid, but there was a half bolt of red polar fleece and some yellowish bric-a-brac. Shelley looked up Flash on her phone and made Aaron point out the best costume. "We could probably make this work," she said, giving the fleece an experimental stretch. "I bet Tawny has a sewing machine."

Aaron was ecstatic, and hugged the bolt of material to his chest, bouncing around. "I'm going to be the Flash!" He demonstrated by running as fast as he could down one of the aisles, and crashed into a display of seed packets. The fabric fell to the floor and unrolled off its cardboard core, while little paper packets of seeds scattered in all directions.

I just quit my job for this, Shelley thought in sudden panic. *What was I thinking?* She clenched her purse in her hands desperately.

"I got it!" Aaron hollered, righting the display. He picked up the seed packets and jammed them back into the wire pockets at random. He stepped on the fabric several times.

"You can't— I just— Let me—" Shelley winced at every creased seed packet and every dirty foot on the fleece and fought her terror back, aware of her lioness' anxious presence. She wasn't going to freak out *now*. She'd been doing so well this week!

She marched down the aisle and began putting the seed packets back in the appropriate pockets. "You can't just jam them in anywhere," she scolded.

Aaron, subdued, handed her the seeds as she worked, and she sorted swiftly. She chose alphabetical because she had no idea what the original organization had been, each variety in its own space, bent corners smoothed. A few of the seed packages were ripped, so Shelley threw them on top of the basket.

"Sorry, Shelley," Aaron said sheepishly, hugging the loose fleece to himself.

"It's okay," Shelley assured him, and herself. "It's all picked up now. We got this."

The merry mood was bruised, and their ice cream and corn dogs were sweating in the warm air as they went back to the cashier.

There *was* a cashier now, at least, a dark-haired, no-nonsense Asian woman who was talking with... the woman who had delivered the casserole. Marta? Was that her name? And here were Shelley and Aaron with a basket full of corn dogs and sugar like a slap in the face.

You're on a roll, Shelley, she told herself sarcastically. *Let's just insult Dean's friends and family and let his kid run wild in the store. Great adulting.*

She briefly considered saying that Bingo had eaten the hapless casserole and then raised her chin defiantly. If Marta didn't mention it, neither would she. She worked well under pressure, Shelley reminded herself firmly. This felt like more pressure than a whole room full of lawyers circling bloody waters as both women turned their eyes to the basket she put defiantly down on the counter.

"You must be Shelley," the cashier said neutrally, picking up the seed packets. It earned her a second look, and Shelley realized she'd managed to get six packets of frilled red cabbage. "I'm Julia."

"A little late for planting," the grey-haired woman said, not commenting on the other contents of Shelley's basket.

"Oh, I don't garden," Shelley said, only hearing how snobby she sounded when the words were out of her mouth. "I knocked over the display and these got damaged."

Aaron stared up at her. Did he really think she would throw him under the bus? It was only an accident.

"You don't *have* to pay for them," Julia said dubiously.

"I insist," Shelley said firmly.

The cashier rang them up at seventy-two cents apiece, then started in on the contents of the basket.

"Shame about Dean's shop," Julia said, shaking her head. "He's worked so hard to keep it running since..."

Both women looked at Shelley and the gray-haired woman asked point blank, "So, did you two meet on the Internet? One of those dating app things?"

"Oh, ah, no," Shelley said. "We met just, last week. I

was here for my Dad's wedding and I needed some... work done on my car." A loose license plate. Shelley made a mental facepalm at the memory.

"Dean's a good mechanic," Julia observed blandly. "Good dad, too."

Shelley was keenly aware of Aaron at her side. She made a generic noise of agreement and wondered if it was a dig on her clear inadequacies.

She kept her chin high. She could do this.

CHAPTER 24

*D*ean opened the door wearily, and was surprised when Bingo failed to come greet him. It was quiet and the light from the TV was flickering in the dim room.

Shelley was sitting at the couch watching the muted TV, and she craned her head around to look at him awkwardly. Dean realized as he walked in that she was pinned down, Bingo on one side of her with his head in her lap, Aaron on the other, asleep against her.

"Help," she mouthed.

"Bingo, down," Dean said quietly.

Bingo kept his head in Shelley's lap and his tail thumped happily.

"Bingo…"

Bingo gave a suffering sigh and oozed off of the couch onto the floor, where he promptly fell over on his side.

Half free, Shelley tried to squirm out from Aaron, freezing when he mumbled and held on.

"I don't want to wake him up," she whispered plaintively.

Dean came around the couch and scooped the un-protesting boy into his arms. "It's amazing what they can sleep through," he whispered back.

Aaron did come awake, though, halfway up the stairs, and mumbled, "You smell bad," into his shoulder. Dean had showered thoroughly at the station, twice, but he knew from experience that the smoky odor and the black pores would remain for a day or more.

His lungs at least felt better, after he'd shifted a few times privately out in the woods.

Aaron fell immediately back to sleep when Dean tucked him into bed, in exactly the position he lay down in.

Dean watched him sleep for a few moments, then trudged back downstairs.

Shelley was picking up the living room; the blankets they'd been wrapped in were folded over the back of the couch and she was putting dirty dishes in the kitchen.

"How did it go?" he asked.

Shelley looked stricken. "Oh, Dean. I did everything wrong. I fed him nothing but junk food, I burnt the corn-dogs, we watched a movie that was way too scary and stayed up long past his bedtime, and I swore in front of him at least six times. I forgot about homework. He ran into a display at the store and I had to buy six packets of frilled red cabbage seeds."

Dean stared. "Frilled red cabbage?"

"I'm a disaster," Shelley said. "I don't know why I thought I could do this. I'm so sorry."

He could feel the tension in her, fear and anxiousness in a tight band around her chest, and he forgot his own problems. "You did great," he said sincerely, pulling her into his arms.

She came willingly, sighing onto his shoulder. "You

should be able to rely on me," she said mournfully. "I wanted to do this right."

"Did he get hurt?"

"No."

"Did he spend the whole night worrying about me?"

"Er, no… We actually had a pretty fun time."

"Have you ever babysat before?"

"Not once."

"And were you great at your first law contract?"

Shelley gave a hiccup of a laugh. "It came back bleeding with markups."

Dean put her at arm's length and looked into her distractingly magical silver eyes. "You did great," he repeated firmly.

She smiled at him and gave a little sniff, blinking fast. "Oh good grief," she said. "Here I am whining about my motherly inadequacies and you just lost your shop. Dean, I'm so sorry. What can I do?"

Dean had managed to forget for a moment, and it all came crashing back at once. Bingo's snore was loud in the quiet room.

"I… don't know," he said, remembering the sour-faced insurance inspector and the way he had pounced on the fact that the fire station wasn't accredited anymore. He remembered Turner, cutting him off the squad in front of the whole town… and Shelley.

"Did they figure out what caused it?" Shelley asked quietly.

Dean shrugged. "It's not official, but there was a power surge reported by the power company shortly before smoke was spotted. Old wiring, a pile of greasy rags or something flammable… they're calling it an accident."

"How bad was the store?"

"Some pretty good smoke damage," Dean said, trying

not to feel pained. "I'll have a fire sale in the fullest meaning of the term."

She gave him a narrow-eyed look that suggested she was picking up on what he was really feeling. "Oh, Dean," she said tenderly. "I hope the insurance doesn't take too long to get it all replaced."

Dean stuffed his doubts down as far as they would go. "I'm sure it will be fine," he lied.

It would have worked with Deirdre, he thought, but Shelley wasn't fooled. She stepped close to him and put her hands gently on his face. "Whatever you need from me, let me know," she said firmly. "I will stuff your kid with junk food and watch inappropriate movies with him anytime you want. Though I may have to buy some earplugs because oh my god, there were times I was afraid he was *never* going to stop talking."

Dean had to laugh. "That's definitely a thing," he agreed. "You get used to it…" Standing so close to her, her hands soft on his cheeks, he was reminded that it had been a whole week since he'd kissed her and it was suddenly very urgent that he make up for that lost time.

"Aaron?" Shelley asked, with a nervous look at the stairs.

"He once slept through a tornado siren," Dean assured her.

She met him with her mouth open, and her arms slid up around his neck. All of her fears and all of his despair melted away in the wave of need and desire that welled up from the pit of his stomach… and places lower.

"I *missed* you," Shelley murmured, when he moved his mouth to her elegant neck.

"I love you," Dean whispered in return.

Bingo was still asleep, so the couch was a safe place to lay her down and peel all of her clothing off.

He kissed every inch of skin as he uncovered it, lingering at her hot, neatly-trimmed pussy as he pushed her tailored pants down over her curvy hips.

"Dean," she cried softly. "Dean!"

He kissed down her long, long legs, even tickling her feet with his tongue as he slipped her socks off.

She giggled, and Bingo gave a groan in his sleep that made them both freeze for a moment.

Then he was stripping off his own pants and coming to cover her... awkwardly, because dog or no dog, the couch proved not to be a particularly comfortable place, and not quite wide enough to accommodate them both. She was hot and wet enough that it didn't matter for the first several thrusts, and she bit back cries of pleasure and scratched his back as she arched to meet him desperately.

They moved briefly to the floor, then scrambled up the stairs as quietly as possible, creeping past Aaron's room like nude thieves.

Then, finally, he was laying her down on the bed and slipping inside her again, where nothing mattered but his bear's demands and her soft cries.

They curled together afterwards, and Dean drew more comfort from her long limbs in his arms than he would have guessed possible. He'd missed her so badly, needed her so deeply...

They dozed for a while, and when he went to get another blanket against the chill of the autumn night, she woke up and touched him. One touch led to another, and another, and the rest of the night was spent in an exhausted blur of making love.

CHAPTER 25

The alarm woke them both entirely too early.

Shelley fumbled at the bedside table with her face still buried in her pillow until Dean finally reached over her and turned off the alarm.

"Didn't your shop burn down yesterday?" she groaned. "Doesn't that at least mean you don't have to get up today?" Then she rolled over, mortified. "Is it too soon to joke?"

"School day," Dean said grimly. "You can sleep. I have to get the slowest kid in the world ready to go."

"I'll get up, too," Shelley said, sitting. She yawned. "We probably should have spent more of last night sleeping."

Dean looked over at her and smiled. His hair was sleep-rumpled and his eyes were tired. "It was worth it," he said, leaning over to kiss her.

"It was worth it," she echoed, when he finally released her.

"I'm going to take a shower," he said with a parting kiss on the forehead.

She lay back on the bed as he left. "I'll be up," she mumbled unconvincingly.

She half-expected to fall back to sleep, but her brain woke up then, and dragged her into a spiral of all the things she'd done wrong. She'd quit her job, she reminded herself, burned her safety net, moved to a town where no one liked her... except Dean and maybe Aaron. But Aaron deserved a better mom, Dean deserved a better mate...

I love you, he'd said, the night before, but did he *really*? Was it just his bear? Was it just the sex? Who could love her?

Too late, Shelley recognized the trap her own mind was leading her into, and a wave of disappointment washed over her. She'd done so well, this entire week, kept herself so together. Having a mate had... *fixed* her, she'd thought. And wasn't sex supposed to cause lots of happy endorphins in the brain? Tears pricked her eyes. Dean didn't know what he'd *really* gotten, and she should just leave now and spare him the heartache of finding out how broken she really was.

It was getting hard to breathe and Shelley could feel her heart pounding irregularly in her chest. She needed one of the pills from her purse, but her purse was downstairs, with her clothes, and it seemed like an impossible distance. Her lioness was looming in her head like a terrifying shadow, angry at her weakness.

Let me help you, she growled.

But Shelley didn't trust her animal's help. Given the choice between flight or fight, she would always run.

"Shelley? Shelley?!"

Dean found her later, half-dressed, sweaty and shaking, sitting on the floor next to the couch with her arms around Bingo, who was utterly delighted to be the center of her attention but less wiggly than usual.

"Are you okay?"

Shelley raised tearful eyes to him. "Not really," she admitted. He was barefoot, hair damp and sticking up in all directions. He was so *beautiful*.

Guilt swamped her. She was supposed to be the one being strong. Dean had just lost his business, his volunteer position. She should be comforting *him*.

Dean settled to a seat beside her and Bingo's little brain nearly exploded with the joy having two of his people so close, abandoning Shelley as she sat up and wiped her tears away. He head-butted Dean, tried to lick him, and when Dean went to gather Shelley into his arms, licked her, and tried to insert himself between them.

Dean shoved him away gently, pulling Shelley into his lap and wrapping his arms around her. "Tell me," he ordered.

"Anxiety," Shelley said into his chest. "Panic attacks. Things shifters aren't supposed to have." She gave a little hiccup of a laugh. "It was fun finding a therapist qualified to diagnose my special case, let me tell you."

"Pretty bad?" Dean prodded. He was making gentle circles with his hands on her back and Shelley could feel the last of her shakes ebb away into the dull, distant aftermath.

She felt numb, like she was wrapped in bubble wrap. Her lioness was a faraway growl and she could feel her body like it wasn't her own. Bingo had his head wedged into the half of her lap he could reach, panting happily.

"Sometimes," she admitted. "I usually get through things and have an attack later, when I'm safe. I have... pills, for when it's really bad. It's kind of a cocktail of prescriptions, because of course I burn things off faster than a human would."

"Of course," Dean agreed.

"I hate them. And… I… thought I was better. I hadn't had an attack since we met, and the anxiety… has been understandable and pretty low key. I thought… maybe I wouldn't do this again. I'd hoped." She'd hoped that finding her mate would magically fix her, she thought with chagrin. Like true love's kiss from a fairy tale.

"You've had a lot of changes, the last week or so," Dean observed.

Shelley was starting to think logically again. "Not as many as you have… but yeah." She gave a humorless chuckle. "I quit my job."

Dean's arms around her tightened in surprise and he was quiet. Doubtful? Angry? Was it too much pressure?

"I could probably get my job back, if things don't work out with us," she promised, glad for the buffer of the drugs. She knew it hurt to think that it might *not* work out, but she didn't *care* that it hurt right now. "You don't have to feel guilty or… obligated or anything. I didn't mean it as a… trap. I just thought that if this was something that was going to happen, it was going to happen all-in. I didn't want this to be just a fling, just a vacation."

"Even with… everything I come with?" Dean's voice was gentle, and Shelley couldn't get a read on his emotions through the muffling effects of the drug.

"Earplugs are cheap and I clearly have my own… baggage. Not that Aaron is baggage," Shelley added swiftly. "He's your son, and I will do my best to love him because you do. I will even try not to swear too much around him or let him watch scary movies. I just… wish I wasn't such a mess. You deserve better. You've got everything figured out, and I drop into your life like a new complication you don't need."

"You are every complication that I need," Dean

murmured near her ear. "And if you think I've got everything figured out, you're sadly mistaken."

"You're a hero," Shelley reminded him.

"I'm an idiot," Dean corrected her. "My businesses are all failing, I'm mortgaged to my ears, I've barely been keeping my own life going. I've spent the last five years trying to be everything for everyone else because I didn't know how to say no to anything... because I had a hole in my life that I didn't know how to fill."

Shelley looked at him, feeling stupid. "You have Aaron."

"And I love Aaron," Dean agreed. "But there are only so many conversations I can have about Legos and farts before I go insane." He paused, and Shelley knew she was supposed to be figuring out what he was trying to say. "You, Shelley. I need *you*. I need your advice, and I need your good sense, and I need your humor and your kisses and that skeptical look you give me when you think I'm making fun of you."

His hand was on her cheek, this thumb making gentle circles. "We don't have to be perfect people to be perfect for each other."

"We're going to make our own life," he said firmly. "Our own future. Together. You and me and your brain, and if you sometimes need to take a pill and sit in a quiet room, I will never love you less for it."

Shelley wasn't aware that she was crying until he wiped the tears away for her, kissing her cheeks tenderly. "I love you, Dean," she said hesitantly. Even through the haze of her pills, she was absolutely sure of it. "I love you, and I will do everything I can to show you that every day."

"Can you help me with insurance forms?" Dean asked, with a crooked smile. "I feel like the world's biggest moron trying to figure out what they are asking for. I'm terrified

I'm going to implicate myself for fraud or something. The adjuster seemed really interested in the fact that the fire department wasn't accredited anymore."

"Oh, yes," Shelley agreed instantly. "I'm great with contracts. And you should hear me on the phone; I will make them tremble in fear. I will squeeze them for every penny they owe you and they will hand it over gratefully."

"Man, I am glad you are on my side," Dean said, dragging a dramatic hand across his brow and Shelley giggled.

She sat up suddenly. "Wait, doesn't Aaron need to get to school? You should be doing that, not dealing with my stupid brain chemistry, shouldn't you?"

"It doesn't matter if he's late," Dean said. "You needed me."

Just like that. As if it was simple. She needed him, and he was there for her.

Shelley was sure it would feel amazing to know that if she weren't being cradled in the comforting dullness that her pill had created. She managed a grateful smile. "I'm okay now. I got this."

"We got this," Dean reminded her, and Shelley felt a well of love and trust breach the wall around her as he kissed her. "I love you…"

Bingo sighed longingly when he was ejected from their laps and they stood up.

"What can I do to help?" Shelley asked.

"Can you make a peanut butter and jelly sandwich?"

"Three ingredients, I think I can manage."

She finished buttoning up her shirt, and went to the kitchen while Dean went upstairs to wake Aaron up.

CHAPTER 26

*A*fter they got a very sleepy and grumbling Aaron off to school with his lunch, Shelley went with Dean to work on the shop inventory and forms.

"You aren't required to answer some of these questions," she told him gravely, flipping through the forms. "They like to throw in all this optional stuff to trip you up. I swear, insurance is one big intimidation game, it's like they're trying to scare you into just not filing."

They talked about the fire department accreditation, too.

"We don't have enough money to keep up with the testing," Dean explained. "We keep things in good shape, we just can't prove it."

Shelley took notes on her phone with a stylus. "I wonder if you'd be eligible for grants," she said thoughtfully. "I'll do some research."

She waded into the ashy shop without hesitating, neatly writing down items that Dean pulled from the burnt wreckage and identified, looking them up on her smartphone and jotting down a current market price.

By the afternoon, they were both sweaty and sooty and Dean thought she had never looked so beautiful.

Her hair was pulled back up into a handkerchief, blonde strands of it sticking to her damp face. If she had started the day with any makeup, it was long gone, and she had a thick black smudge across one cheek that Dean didn't want to tell her about.

Various neighbors wandered in and out while they were working, commenting on the general awful state of things, sympathizing with the workload and the loss, speculating on the damage that might have been done, and without fail, offering to help with the cleanup.

Shelley shook her head in warning. "Don't clean up until the claim is settled," she warned. "It's all evidence."

She got many curious, speculative looks. Even her black cheek smudge and dirty clothes couldn't make her look less out of place.

He caught her frowning down at her shoes when everyone was gone, sitting on the sidewalk. They were smudged and scuffed.

"They're probably never going to be clean again," he said apologetically, handing her a lukewarm diet cola from the hardware store vending machine. The structure didn't have any power yet.

"They're just shoes," Shelley said firmly, as if she was trying to convince herself. She took a drink of her soda, grimaced at the temperature, and followed it with a thirsty second sip.

"Thank you," Dean said sincerely, popping the top to a warm root beer. "You didn't have to do this."

Shelley bumped shoulders with him. "I'm good at filling out paperwork," she said with a crooked smile.

"We make a good team," Dean told her.

The black smudge on her cheek hitched up with her

smile.

They called it a day shortly before Aaron was due to get off of school and Shelley took the first shower.

Dean was shaking ash off of his pants on the porch when Deirdre pulled up with an out of character shriek of her car brakes.

She stomped up from the curb and Dean caught her wiping angry tears off her face.

"Dammit Dean! They said you charged in without turnout gear! That you could have been killed! What were you thinking, Dean? Did you think about what that could do to Aaron if you'd died?"

"I wasn't killed." Dean kept his voice calm and reasonable. "I'm fine."

Deirdre gave a little whimper, and Dean automatically opened his arms. She stepped close to hug him, and he could feel her sigh against him. "Oh, Dean, I was so worried."

"I'm fine," he assured her. "I'm *fine.*"

"I'm so sorry about the shop," she mumbled into his shirt. "It's not fair."

He was just thinking that her embrace felt so much different than Shelley's did, and that the strangest part was that Deirdre's was the one that didn't feel normal anymore, when Deirdre froze and then backed away from him.

"Shelley," she said carefully.

Barefoot, Shelley's approach had been cat-silent, and she was standing just inside the screen door. The black smudge was gone from her cheek and her hair was still damp around her face.

"Deirdre," Shelley replied, just as carefully.

Deirdre scuffed one foot along the porch. "I... ah... actually came a little early because I wanted to see if you wanted to grab a coffee at the bakery before I took Aaron home." Her voice suggested that she didn't expect Shelley to accept.

Dean could feel the prickly anxiety from Shelley, but he wasn't surprised when she nodded solemnly. "I'd like that," she said evenly. "Let me get some shoes."

"Sorry," Deirdre said sheepishly, when Shelley disappeared. "I hope I didn't make things... awkward by giving you a hug."

Dean had to laugh. "Awkward is kind of a running theme. We'll manage."

Deirdre chewed on her lower lip. "Are you... happy?"

The approach of Shelley's clicking heels prevented Dean from answering. The screen door swung closed after her with a bang, and she only hesitated a moment before stepping close to give him a swift goodbye kiss. Dean caught her face in his hands to make it slightly more than a utilitarian peck and there was a soft, real smile at her lips when she stepped back.

Deirdre looked delighted. "Oh, I'm so glad we're doing this," she chattered. "I've got so many questions, I'll try not to pry, and I've got so many stories to tell you about Dean! Do you mind if we walk? It's just a couple of blocks and isn't it a gorgeous day? I just love autumn, with all the colors and it's not so hot anymore, and of course, it's nearly Halloween, which is my favorite holiday. What's your favorite holiday, Shelley?"

Dean knew Deirdre was covering her nervousness with her babble, and it struck him that she was very different from Shelley, who tended to retreat to distant silence and formality when faced with the same stresses. Then he realized that he was watching his ex-wife walk away with his new girlfriend with the sole purpose of getting to know each other better and he had a moment of sudden dread.

This was a *terrible* idea.

CHAPTER 27

"Have you had the pastries here yet? They're really amazing. Better than Clausen's, even, if you've ever been there. Of course, Clausen's doesn't have coffee, or a place to sit. I'm sorry, I'm just non-stop, you've barely got a word in edgewise, do you know what you want to order?"

Shelley had more sympathy for Deirdre than the other woman probably imagined. She was clearly very nervous, and just as determined to be friendly.

There was no line, and Shaun was behind the counter wiping off the espresso machine.

"A cinnamon roll and a…"

"Latte," Shaun finished for her. "Are you two together?"

"Yes," Shelley said, just as Deirdre said, "No."

"I'll get this," Shelley insisted.

Deirdre blushed. "You have to let me get the next one," she said. "An Americano and one of the cherry-filled danishes. Messy," she said to Shelley, "but worth it."

"For here?" Shaun asked with a grin.

"Yes," Shelley and Deirdre said together. Deirdre and Shaun were eyeing each other curiously, clearly trying to decide who the other person was and Shelley finally gave a sigh as Shaun passed plates over with their pastries. "Shaun is my brother," she explained. "He moved to Green Valley a little over a year ago and married Andrea. Shaun, this is Deirdre. Dean's ex-wife."

"Oh," they each said knowingly. "Oh."

"You must be Trevor's dad! Aaron talks about him all the time. It's nice to meet you," Deirdre said brightly, and they exchanged a handshake over the counter.

"You, too," Shaun answered, bemused. "I'll bring your coffees out."

They were the only customers, and they took the seat furthest from the counter, looking out the window.

"This used to be a general store when I was a kid," Deirdre offered, using a fork to take a bite of her danish. "And see that big brick building on the corner? That used to be a bank. Marta lives there now, and the inside is amazing. It still has the teller cages and her closet is in the old vault. Giant, tall ceilings, and marble everywhere."

"Green Valley is a really sweet little town," Shelley offered. Shaun's baking was as good as she remembered; the cinnamon roll was light and fluffy, with sticky, delicious filling. He had sprinkled nuts on top without asking, remembering that she liked them.

"Emphasis on little," Deirdre said with a wince. "I… don't know what Dean told you. Or what anyone else has told you…"

Shelley was too busy feeling sorry for Deirdre to be nervous herself. "He told me," she said sympathetically. She leaned forward. "He's…"

"Your coffees," Shaun said, setting steaming cups in front of them. Like the entire image of the shop, they were cute and quaintly mis-matched. "I'll be closing up, but it will take me a while to finish in back, so don't let me rush you."

"Thanks," Deirdre said, and as soon as he had gone in back, she leaned forward avidly. "Dean's what now?"

"My mate," Shelley said, and just hearing the words raised a wave of satisfaction and peace in her.

"I knew it!" Deirdre crowed. "He wouldn't come out and say it, but it's obvious you're a shifter, and there was just something about the way you looked at each other." She lifted her cup and toasted a bemused Shelley. "I am so happy for you both."

She seemed greatly relieved and far less nervous after that, and Shelley found herself letting her guard down as they chatted. Just as she'd promised, Deirdre did have embarrassing stories about Dean in childhood, and Shelley shyly asked questions about Aaron that opened absolute floodgates.

"He tried to explain a game to me yesterday and do you sometimes not understand him even though he's using perfectly clear English words?" Shelley asked. "Because he was telling me about it for probably thirty minutes and I knew less about it at the end than I did at the beginning."

Deirdre held her sides and laughed. "That is completely normal," she assured Shelley.

They talked about the food he liked (nearly everything), and the tricks that Deirdre employed to get him to do chores and go to bed.

"He's allergic to cats," Deirdre added, and Shelley was glad she'd already drunk most of her coffee, because she startled and the contents of her cup sloshed to the edge.

"Probably not big cats," Deirdre said with a grin. "Tiger?"

131

"Lion," Shelley confessed, finding herself smiling in return.

"I'm a deer," Deirdre said cheerfully. "Which is a little easier, if you ask me. I got caught in our backyard last year, and it's a lot easier to explain a deer than it is an exotic wild animal. I just pretended to eat some flowers and was glad it wasn't hunting season. My neighbor posted photos on Facebook and I tagged myself before I realized that was a bad idea."

"I don't get a lot of chances to shift in the city," Shelley said wistfully. "That's one advantage to Green Valley. Lots of forest around here to go running in."

"Madison isn't too bad. Plenty of parks."

They talked until Shelley was sure that Shaun was regretting his invitation not to feel rushed and the sun outside was starting to set.

"Oh gosh," Deirdre finally said. "I bet Aaron's been home for ages and the boys are wondering where on earth we are."

Shelley left a generous tip and they walked outside.

"Do you mind if we walk the long way around?" Deirdre asked. "I... wanted to go by and see the shop. What's left of it."

It wasn't quite as alarming with the garage door down as it had been with the charred interior exposed. Black smoke stains around every entrance and vent only hinted at the damage inside.

"He was working there when we were both in high school," Deirdre observed, subdued. "He talked about going to school for engineering. He could have gotten a sports scholarship, but he didn't think it was fair because he was a shifter. He's always thinking about everyone else, you know. And later, when we were thinking about it again, suddenly Aaron."

"He's... a great kid," Shelley said, guessing she ought to say something.

Deirdre flashed her a swift look. "The best," she agreed, and her mouth was firm and without a trace of regret.

"I... I don't know a lot about kids," Shelley said, as if it wasn't the most obvious thing in the world. "He'll... probably come home with new swear words and bad habits, so I'm sorry in advance for that."

Deirdre's eyes softened and she laughed. "You'll do fine," she promised. "Aaron already thinks you're 'okay, I guess,' which is more enthusiastic than he gets about most people."

"I'll take 'okay, I guess,'" Shelley chuckled.

"If you need anything, just let me know," Deirdre said warmly. "I didn't know a thing about kids, either, and honestly, you just make it up as you go. They're a lot more resilient than you might think."

"Thank you," Shelley said genuinely. "I really appreciate that."

They walked around the back side of the shop, where the damage was more apparent: the back wall had been eaten clean through by fire at the top, the roof noticeably missing in places. Charred bones of the structure held up a blue tarp that rustled in the autumn wind, bright against the soot darkening everything else.

"It could have been a lot worse," Deirdre said practically, as they came back around the front.

Shelley wondered if that was the Green Valley motto.

They walked quietly back to Dean's house and paused at the curb before going in.

"Oh," Shelley said, suddenly remembering. "I offered to make Aaron a Halloween costume. He wanted to be

Flash, we've bought fabric. I don't know if you'd planned anything…"

"Oh, that's wonderful," Deirdre said, to Shelley's relief. "I would have picked something up last minute at the store. It wouldn't have lasted five minutes into trick-or-treating. If I could have even found a Flash costume. Seven hundred ice queen costumes, a billion Batmans…"

"Lots of options if he wanted to be a sexy nurse," Shelley said dryly. "Even here."

Deirdre laughed. "You should get one of those for yourself," she suggested with a wink. "Dean would love it."

Shelley felt her cheeks heat.

"I like you," Deirdre said frankly. "I'm so terribly glad that Dean met you and I'm so happy to have you as a… er… step-ex?"

"I'm really happy to have you as a… step-ex, too," Shelley confessed.

"Moooooom!" Aaron was a small blue streak, accompanied by Bingo, who had only just noticed them when Aaron did and was barking twice as much to make up for it. The screen door was still slamming shut when the two reached them.

Aaron flung his arms around Deirdre and Bingo tried to lick her, then moved to Shelley, who patted him sedately on the head. "Dad's shop burned down, Mom! Did you know? The kids at school say it was a trad-egy and that Dad's a hero even if he's not a *super*hero and Trevor says they're going to give him a parade and Clara said that was stupid and the teacher told her not to say stupid and I'm hungry and did you bring me a cookie from the bakery?"

CHAPTER 28

*H*andoff was always a measure of chaos, and Dean could not figure out how Shelley, with all her outward serenity, seemed to make it louder and more crazy just by being there. It took a solid twenty minutes of packing snacks for the drive and remembering a favorite stuffy that had to be brought and there was laughter and Deirdre was teasing them both without remorse and Bingo was so excited by everything that Dean worried his little dog brain was going to explode.

Finally, they were waving Deirdre and Aaron away down the quiet street and Bingo, exhausted, herded them back into the house and lay down at the threshold like a doorstop.

"Did you have a good cup of coffee?"

"It was good," Shelley assured him. "What's with the boxes?"

Dean grinned. "I'll show you."

He took her hand and led her to the back of the house. "This was my mom's sewing room. I thought you should have it. I don't have a lot of closet space upstairs, but there's another closet down here, and you should have your own space."

He'd only gotten about half of the boxes moved out. "I've been using this to store stuff my folks didn't want when they moved, and I just never got around to getting rid of it."

It was a sunny little room, looking out over the backyard. Blackberries had grown up and were filling in the bottom of the windows.

Shelley was quiet.

"We could... look for another house if you'd rather," Dean said. It was a pretty small room, and a small closet. Shelley was probably used to spacious apartments with matching furniture and coordinating decor. "I mean, once the insurance is settled." Probably she had enough of her own money to outright buy a house. There was so much they hadn't talked about.

"I love it," she said in a very small voice. Her hands were trembling and Dean realized that some of the tension he was feeling was hers, bubbling up.

Dean swept her into his arms without pausing to think about it. "What can I do?" he asked. "Do you need a pill?"

She turned in his embrace and sighed into him. "No," she said. "This is perfect. This is absolutely perfect. Just hold me."

They stood that way for an unmeasured time and he could feel her settle. "I'm sorry you have to have to deal with my stupid brain," she said, muffled in his chest.

"We don't use the word stupid in this house," he scolded her, just as if she was Aaron. Then he kissed the top of her head and added, "Besides, it's no hardship to have an extra excuse to hold onto you. You tell your brain to do whatever it needs to."

She smiled up at him. "I don't know about my brain,

but the rest of me is exactly where I want to be." Her hands slipped up around his neck.

Dean leaned over and kissed her, slowly and full of promise. "We can live anywhere you want," he said seriously, drawing back. "Maybe… maybe the fire at the garage was a good reminder. It's just stuff. And this is just a place. We can be a family anywhere we go, anywhere we choose to be, whatever we decide to do. This is our chance to redefine our lives, make a new start. Yours and mine. Together."

Shelley looked at him so warmly, her silvery eyes full of wonder, that Dean wanted to drown in them. "Together," she agreed. "*Here*."

"It's a small house," Dean warned. "It's a small *town*."

"Then you'll never be very far away from me," Shelley said softly.

Then his mouth was on hers, and her arms were around his neck and he was perfectly, absolutely home.

CHAPTER 29

*S*ure enough, Tawny did have a sewing machine, and she was more than happy to set it up for Shelley.

"I haven't unpacked this since we moved," the gray-haired woman said, putting it out on the desk in the spare room. "I'll show you how to thread it... if I remember."

"I've got it," Shelley said, popping the bobbin out and looping the thread around the pick-up hook.

"You know your way around a sewing machine," Tawny said with surprise.

"Why is everyone shocked when I can do something domestic?" Shelley asked more sharply than she intended. "I like nice clothing. Sometimes I make my own."

"Ever thought about going into fashion design?" Tawny asked innocently.

"It's not practical," Shelley said dismissively.

"Not everything has to be practical," Tawny said and Shelley gave her a wry sideways look because Tawny was the absolute epitome of a practical, down-to-earth grandmother. Shelley doubted she had ever done anything impulsive in her life.

She wondered if Tawny had talked to Damien; Shelley had once dreamed about working in fashion. Did her father even *know* that?

They set up the machine and Shelley lay the fabric out with the pattern pinned on top. It all looked adorably small and she held it up several times as she worked, bemused that someone so short could be so full of life as Aaron was.

Tawny offered to help and Shelley graciously accepted. Tawny cut the top while Shelley sewed the bottoms.

"I was looking at kids costumes online," she said. "You can find some really nice handmade costumes, but they are expensive, and it seems like a lot of investment into a one-time costume for a kid that will grow out of in a few months."

"I think that's why those cheap, disposable costumes are so popular," Tawny observed, adding a sleeve to Shelley's pile.

"It seems like there ought to be some kind of middle ground," Shelley mused. "A well-made costume that doesn't cost the world. Maybe with hems you can let out as they grow?" She held up the pants, which she had deliberately made longer than Aaron's measurements. They could be tacked up for now, and let out as he got taller.

"That's a great idea," Tawny agreed.

"I didn't think to get elastic," Shelley said, when the bottoms were otherwise finished; she wouldn't hem them until she had a chance to try them on Aaron.

"I'm sure I have some," Tawny said. "Let's see…"

That led to dismantling an entire closet of boxes containing fabric. "I should make your father something out of this," Tawny laughed, holding up a folded square of bright yellow fabric with cartoon bees all over it.

"That... doesn't look like Dad," Shelley said skeptically, biting off an extra string from the pajama shirt she had just put together.

"It's an inside joke," Tawny explained. "Your father is allergic to bees."

Shelley stared. "I had no idea. I didn't realize shifters *could* be."

"He went into anaphylactic shock right in front of me," Tawny recounted. "Collapsed right in my living room. I've never been so frightened."

"What did you do?" Shelley asked curiously. 911 wasn't exactly an option for shifters.

"He shifted. He explained that shifting can cause muscles and bones to heal, so there was no reason that it shouldn't also help stop an over-active histamine response."

"And it worked?"

"He was right as rain, in just a few minutes. Faster than a shot of epinephrine."

Shelley knew the trick for healing faster after shifting, but she hadn't imagined that the process would apply to the more complex parts of the body. "Curious," she said, filing away the information. "Oh, that's perfect!"

Tawny was holding up a strip of white elastic, excavated from the bottom of a bin.

"I'll take this with me," Shelley said. "And I can put that in by hand and pin all the cuffs for sewing tomorrow once I've had a chance to try this on him."

She glanced at the clock. School didn't get out for another hour, but she wanted to be sure to be there when Aaron came home. Dean was working late at the store to get ready for the fire sale and Shelley was already feeling anxious about helping Aaron do his homework and keeping him fed and entertained.

"This is a good stopping place, can I come back

tomorrow morning and finish these up?" Shelley folded up the pants and shirt with the loose elastic.

"That sounds like a great plan," Tawny agreed. "He's going to love them."

"I hope so," Shelley said fervently.

She got back to Dean's house in plenty of time—her house? Could she think of it as her own? As *theirs*? Certainly nowhere else Shelley had ever been had felt as much like *home*.

But Aaron didn't come home. Shelley paced the house until Bingo whined at her anxiously, and the clock ticked past the time she had expected him… and then ten minutes past that.

She checked her phone, even knowing that Dean's phone still wasn't working, and wondered when it was acceptable to open a search with the police.

Finally, when Aaron was officially fifteen minutes late, she called her brother Shaun's number.

"Welcome to the zoo," Andrea answered the phone merrily. "How can I direct your call?"

"Hi Andrea," Shelley said, feeling the tightness of worry in her chest and the panic that was starting to make her breathe funny. "I was just wondering if Aaron had come home with Trevor. I…" I've lost him, Shelley thought in horror. I've lost Dean's son and proved that I'm the worst mother ever. "He was supposed to come straight home, but he never showed up." She sounded as hysterical as she was starting to feel.

"I haven't seen him," Andrea said, sobering. "Hang on, let me go see if Trevor knows anything."

Shelley concentrated on breathing, running through all the meditation tricks in her mental bag. She wasn't going to freak out. She was going to think logically. She was going to find Aaron and strangle him (just a little) for making her worry so much and then they'd laugh and everything would be fine.

"Shelley?"

"I'm here, I'm here!" Shelley almost shouted into her phone. "Does he know where Aaron is?"

"He says they had a fight and Aaron went to the place where Trevor was practicing shifting. Do you know what that is?"

Shelley blinked, remembering their outing—had it really only been two weeks ago? "Yes, I know where that is."

"Do you need any help?"

I need *Dean*, Shelley thought. But she could do this. She scrawled a note to Dean and left it on the table. "No, I'll just drive up there and see if I can find him first. He can't have gotten very far yet."

It was a few blocks from school to the deserted property they'd gone running in. Aaron was fast, but he wasn't that fast. He couldn't have gotten very deep into the forest in such a short time. Could he?

"Call me when you find him," Andrea said firmly. "If I haven't heard from you in half an hour, I'll send out the cavalry."

"Thank you, Andrea!" Shelley was already at her car when she hung up, making a swift, squeaking-tire spin in the middle of the deserted street to point herself in the right direction.

It was cold, and the friendly, warm sun of the past few days was hidden in a gray bank of clouds that threatened snow. There were more leaves on the ground now than there were on the trees, and they swirled away from Shelley's car as she drove down the isolated drive.

As she pulled up at the trailhead, she had a moment of doubt. What if Aaron was just now arriving home, confused because no one was there? She reminded herself firmly that if he was, the house was warm and full of food. But if he was here, if he'd gotten lost, he would be cold and hungry.

She closed her car door and stood in the chilly air for a long moment, listening and scenting. Her senses were not as good when she wasn't a lion, but they were still better than a normal human's, by a long shot.

There was a strong scent on the breeze. *A bear*, her lion supplied.

Had Aaron successfully shifted, the way he'd always wanted to?

Shelley walked into the woods, confident in her ability to retrace her steps, and followed her nose and her ears. Several times, she questioned her choice to stay in human form—she'd be better at this as a lion. But she didn't want to terrify Aaron.

They'd had a talk, the three of them, about Shelley being a lion shifter like Trevor—another of those conversations that wasn't covered in any mommy blogs or child care manuals. But knowing she was a lion was a lot different than coming across one in the woods

She heard him snuffling at last, and was, for once, grateful for his non-stop running nose.

He was sitting in the center of a tiny clearing, not quite crying, but looking very close to it.

"Aaron!" Shelley cried in relief, running the last few steps to drop to her knees beside him. "Are you okay? I've been looking for you!"

"I wanted to be a bear," Aaron explained. "Or even a deer, like Mommy. Trevor gets to shift, and I want to. He showed me this is where he comes, and I thought maybe I could…"

"You shouldn't ever come by yourself," Shelley scolded

143

as she checked him over. There were scratches on his face and his hands, and he looked cold and dirty, but he seemed unharmed. "You have to ask. Someone grown up should *always* come here with you."

Aaron's chin quivered and he stared at his filthy tennis shoes. "I didn't want to ask you," he said sheepishly. "Because…"

"Because you heard that I didn't like kids," Shelley guessed with a stab of guilt. Dean had told her about what Shaun had said and about the conversation he'd had with Aaron afterwards.

Aaron didn't say anything, continuing to stare down.

"Aaron," Shelley said, her voice breaking. "Aaron, I may not be great with other kids, but I… I like *you*. I want *you* to ask me for things. Like your Halloween costume, or whatever. I want… I want to be your mom. Not to replace your mom, of course, just… could you ever think of me as family? Because I'd really like that."

She wasn't prepared for him to look up at her, tears in his hazel eyes, and then throw his arms around her neck, and she almost fell backwards from the force of it before folding her arms around him.

He was so slight and fragile in her embrace. Shelley held him tight, burying her face in his curls and willed her heartbeat to slow. He was okay, he was safe, and everything was going to be *fine*.

"We can be a team," Aaron said near her ear. "Team Aaron and Shelley."

Then he gave a little squeak. "Dad!" he cried, squirming out of Shelley's arms, just as the hair on the back of her neck rose in alarm.

Shelley turned to find a bear snuffling its way out of the brush, nose in the air.

"Aaron, wait!" Shelley cried, as Aaron started to run towards it. "That's not your dad!"

Wild bears in the fall should be fat and sleepy, but this bear was skinny, with a ragged coat, and its eyes were anything but sleepy. This was a hungry bear, maybe sick, and it had a bead on Aaron, who had stopped in confusion halfway to it.

"Don't run!" Shelley yelped too late.

Aaron, realizing the danger he was in, turned on his heel and bolted back for Shelley.

The bear, its hunting instinct triggered by the small, soft prey fleeing it, charged forward with unexpected speed...

...and was met by a snarling lioness as Shelley shifted, shreds of her clothing scattering in a flurry of silk and linen.

Shelley's unsheathed claws slashed across the bear's face, before the greater bulk of the bear bowled her over. It roared at her, striking with heavy clawed paws and Shelley snapped her teeth, trying to get a grip on its sensitive nose. She had to stay between it and Aaron, she *had* to protect him.

Shelley was so focused on keeping Aaron safe, on driving the bear away from him, that she was incautious in her attacks, and the canny bear struck back, sinking teeth into her shoulder.

She roared in shock, then turned to bite back, able only to reach an ear from the angle of the hold the bear had on her. She twisted to claw at the bear's neck and belly and the bear bellowed in pain and released her.

Both of them scrambled to their feet and faced off, Shelley circling deliberately so that she was once again in front of Aaron. She was limping.

The bear snuffled and swung its head back and forth,

clearly trying to decide if the temptation of the prey was worth fighting the lioness. He outweighed Shelley considerably, but wasn't as healthy or as fast. They were both bleeding, Shelley in sluggish lines from the place he'd locked his teeth, the bear from a dozen deep scratches and one torn ear. His injuries were largely cosmetic, but Shelley was clearly more invested in the outcome of the battle. She raised her head and roared a challenge, her tail lashing.

It was too much for the injured bear and he turned and shuffled back into the brush that he'd come from.

Shelley sat stiffly, and let her lioness twist to lick her injured shoulder while she decided what to do next.

"Sh-shelley?"

Shelley swung her head to see Aaron, eyes filled with frightened tears, arms clutched around himself. "Sh-shelley?" he repeated.

Shelley padded slowly up to him, and gave him a gentle head-butt. She was much larger as a lion than he was, but he fearlessly held his ground, and when Shelley leaned her big head against him, he wrapped his arms around her.

She licked him, and he giggled. "Ow," he protested. "Your tongue is scratchy!"

They stayed that way a moment, Aaron hugging into the thick fur of her neck, Shelley leaning into his embrace. It was starting to snow.

"Your clothes got all ruined," Aaron observed sorrowfully. "They were so fancy."

Shelly shrugged, then pulled away. They needed to get back to the parking lot and she needed to find something to wear before they both got hypothermia. When Aaron started to walk beside her, she stepped in front of him. He tried to go around her, but she cut him off again.

Figure it out, she willed at him.

His eyes got big. "Can I ride you?" he asked enthusiastically.

Shelley let her jaw go loose in a big cat grin and nodded her head.

Lions were not built as riding animals, but Aaron was barely a burden, and he quickly figured out how to sit and where to hold on so that Shelley could carry him swiftly back to the parking lot, following her path by scent back the way they'd come.

CHAPTER 30

*D*ean pulled into the wide spot at the end of the drive, swearing and fighting down panic. It was starting to snow, very lightly, and he almost slipped stepping out of the truck. Shelley's car was already there.

"Aaron!" he hollered desperately. "Aaron!" Shelley's hasty note only said she was coming to look for Aaron here, no details about why Aaron would be here or why she had to look for him.

There were no signs of either of them. Not signs he could follow as a human.

He was unbuttoning his shirt and still struggling out of his work boots when he heard a distant, "Dad?"

Staying in human form, he ran towards the voice, and after a moment, met Aaron on a narrow trail, riding a limping lioness. "Dad!"

Dean's heart nearly stopped as he realized that they were both covered in blood.

Then the lioness was shaking Aaron gently off her back and shifting into Shelley, naked and shivering. "It's my blood, don't worry," she said, standing stiffly. "It's already healing."

Since his shirt was already half unbuttoned, he took it off the rest of the way and helped her, wincing, into it.

"Dad! She fought a bear! It was amazing! It was all rarrrrgh and whoosh and scary and Shelley roars way better than Trevor and it was really scary and can I go home now?"

"What were you doing out here?" Dean demanded, gathering the boy into his arms. Aaron was shivering, but seemed unharmed.

"I wanted to come practice trying shifting," Aaron whined. "I'm sorry. I should have asked... but you were busy and I was scared to ask Shelley."

Dean exchanged a look with Shelley.

She looked back at him and smiled, her silver eyes filled with relief. "We're good now."

"We're a team," Aaron agreed.

"Well, team," Dean said, almost shaky with relief. "What do you say we head home and have a snack and take hot showers?"

"Can I have a bath?" Aaron suggested.

"You boys go ahead," Shelley said. "I'm going to shift again and heal up the worst of these bite marks. I don't want to get rabies from some wild bear if I can help it."

"What's rabies?" Aaron wanted to know. "Is it like babies? Eeewwwwwww!"

Dean gave her a swift kiss and tried to buckle Aaron into his booster seat. "I can do it Dad, geez. I'm *seven*." Torn between wanting to scold him some more and wanting to crush him in a hug, Dean stopped fussing over Aaron and went around to the driver's seat. "See you soon," he said to Shelley.

He drew Aaron a bath as soon as they got home,

reminded him about splashing on the floor, and piled toys into the water with him.

He got downstairs just as Shelley pulled up. She looked around furtively, then dashed to the door, still wearing nothing more than his shirt. She was holding her purse and a large bundle of red material in her arms. Dean could only imagine the stories that was going to spark.

He caught her in his arms just inside the door, and Bingo bounced around them, barking and wagging his tail because all of his people were back where they belonged.

"Do you need something?" he asked. "A pill? You said the attacks usually happened after the stress, when you were safe again. Would a back rub help?"

"I'm fine," Shelley said, embracing him awkwardly with her arms full of fabric. "I'm... actually fine." She stepped back and looked at him with glowing eyes. "I'll show you." She put the things she'd been holding down on the table and unbuttoned his flannel shirt. The bite marks on her shoulder looked like old scabs now, or fresh scars. There was still dried blood on her skin.

"When I shift, it heals things up, right? Like, if you're defying physics and changing into a completely new body, it's going to make it the *right* new body, all healed up." She tapped her forehead. "This, this is a chemical imbalance. Tricky to treat, more complicated than just muscles and skin, but still, the body not quite working right. And when I shift, it *fixes* things. That's why I felt so great and in control after our first date—I'd gone running with my Dad and Trevor just the night before."

She laughed and shook her head. "My lioness kept telling me that she could help, but I was sure that her idea of *help* was to turn into a lion and eat someone. I didn't even consider that she could *actually* help me."

"You beautiful, clever, brave, wonderful woman," Dean said.

Her arms were free again, so Dean swept her up into a less encumbered hug, and added a probing kiss to it.

"I don't think this is a permanent fix," Shelley warned as they broke apart. "I mean, I really want it to be, but there will probably be times I don't recognize what is happening, or can't shift for some reason."

"I love you and all your quirks," Dean promised. "And even if this isn't a fix-all, I will still love you."

She sagged into him embrace, full of relief and gratitude.

"My water is cold!"

Aaron was standing at the bottom of the stairs wrapped in a towel.

"Let's get you dried off and dressed for bed!" Dean let go of Shelley and she buttoned his shirt back up over herself.

"Oh, wait! Before you get dressed, I want you to try on your costume!" She walked to the table and unfolded the fabric to reveal a hooded pajama set trimmed in gold bric-a-brac. "I've got the logo patches on expedited order for the front and for the lightning bolts above the ears. They should be here tomorrow for the finishing touches. I just want to get the cuff lengths right. We'll tuck up the extra so you can let it out when you get taller."

"That looks great," Dean said, impressed. He didn't know much about sewing or design, but the costume looked well made.

Aaron frowned, and reluctantly tried it on. It fit him perfectly, with just enough room in the armpits that he'd be able to run around easily, and Shelley pinned up the legs and arms. She tightened the elastic at the waist and safety pinned it, then sat back on her heels.

"Well?" she asked. "Do you like it?"

Aaron petted the soft material and traced some of the trim. "It's... nice."

Shelley looked confused and then her face shuttered to her boardroom mask. "Okay," she said patiently. "What would make it better?"

Aaron chewed on his lip and finally said. "I don't want to be The Flash. I want to be Iron Man!"

"You *said* you wanted to be The Flash," Shelley said in disbelief.

"Yeah, but I changed my mind because Iron Man can fly and blow things up."

"But... I made you a *Flash* costume," Shelley protested.

That was the point at which Dean could no longer hold his laughter in. "Aaron, why don't you get out of that now and go get into your sleeping PJs."

"But I'm huuuuunnnnnngggggry," Aaron protested, wriggling out of the costume with Shelley's help.

"You can eat dinner in pajamas," Dean promised him, still chuckling. "Wait, take your wet towel and hang it on the rack in the bathroom."

He knew there was an even chance that the towel would be found on the bedroom floor.

Shelley had a mixed expression of betrayal and bemusement on her face once Aaron had skipped up the stairs.

"Welcome to parenting," Dean said, unable to keep from grinning at her. "Please don't kill him."

"I spent $23 for the expedited shipping," she said in frustration. "This is a bait and switch!"

Dean tucked a piece of stray hair behind her ear. "We'll have a bit of a talk before bed about being grateful and he'll probably draw you a few apology cards. But he's also seven, so it's... a work in progress."

Shelley pulled up her phone with a sigh and began googling photos of Iron Man. "I can probably order a new patch that looks like that glowy chest thing, and we can put on some gold mechanical looking bits on the sleeves and legs. Some red gloves, maybe? It will be hard to match that red."

"You're a good sport," Dean said sincerely.

Shelley looked up from her phone and gave him a crooked smile. "I have good reasons to put in the work," she said warmly. "Two of them, at least."

Bingo groaned to his feet from where he'd been laying and trotted to get in on whatever activity he might have slept through, tail wagging.

"Three reasons," Shelley amended, ruffling his ears.

She put her phone down as Dean gathered her into his arms again and kissed her. She was still wearing only his flannel shirt and her hair was still damp from the snow.

"So worth the work," she murmured in his ear as he kissed down her neck. "Can I eat dinner wearing my pajamas, too?"

"Pajamas for all!" Dean declared magnanimously.

Hand in hand, they went upstairs to change. Aaron met them at the top of the stairs, dressed in his favorite pajamas. "Are you going to kiss?" he demanded in disgust.

"Probably a lot," Dean said cheerfully.

"Ugh, ew! Gross!" Aaron mimed throwing up, or possibly choking; the particulars were uncertain, but the disgust was clear.

EPILOGUE

*T*he shrieks of two happy children playing echoed across the spring lawn as they went hunting for Easter eggs. Bingo barked, romping with them. Trees were just starting to bud overhead, and early flowers were coming up in the beds.

"I think that your costumes are a success," Dean said to Shelley as she put their crockpot down on the table on Shaun's porch. "That is the sound of utter delight."

"I'm never going to get Trevor out of it again," Andrea lamented, bringing out a plate of cookies and a stack of napkins.

Aaron was wearing a blue costume, Trevor a red one. They were, at a glance, wearing simple, bright colored pajamas, but each garment was completely reversible. One side of the fabric was plain, the other printed with mechanical patterns. Cleverly placed Velcro, snaps, buttons, and zippers allowed the application of superhero logos, capes, and accessories so that each outfit could have dozens of costume variations.

Currently, Trevor was dressed as Superman on the top,

with mechanical wrist braces, cyborg legs, and no cape. Aaron had the Iron Man gloves, but was otherwise dressed as the Flash, with a cape of his own waving behind him as he streaked across the lawn in search of the hidden Easter loot.

Shelley personally thought they'd have a lot more luck finding the eggs if they slowed down and actually looked for them, but they were having so much fun that it was hard to criticize their methods, even if their baskets were empty.

"Those turned out wonderfully," Tawny said. She was carrying a platter of vegetables and devilled eggs, and she put them on the potluck table on the porch. "Such clever touches! They'll be able to imagine up their own superhero combinations."

"We're getting the licensing finalized this week and the workshop in Minneapolis should have them in production by the end of next month," Shelley said, feeling shyly pleased. "And did you see? The cuffs all unfold so you can get an extra three inches out of the arms and legs. It's good fabric, and quality stitching, plus all machine wash and dry."

"Nice work, Shelley-bean," her father said approvingly. He was carrying a platter of ham and Bingo was drooling and cavorting at his heels.

"They're talking about a line for girls, too," Shelley said, grinning, as Damien set his tray on the table with the other food. "A princess, fairy, witch line, as well as a super-heroine set. It will have a little skirt, a cape that is just as long as the boys' capes, bracelets, a crown... I'm really excited to start on it."

"They're very practical," Tawny teased, handing her a carrot stick. Shelley took it automatically, then didn't know what to do with it.

"How's school going, Dean?" Damien asked.

"Fine," Dean said, sounding embarrassed. "Lots of math."

"He says *fine*," Shelley added with a snort. "He's top of all his correspondence classes, he's finished two of them early, and his mentor says he wishes his other students had half his work ethic. He's already saying that Dean can test out of some of the engineering intro classes." They had decided to close the shop rather than rebuild it, and the insurance settlement had been generous enough to cover several semesters of school.

Dean actually blushed, which Shelley found utterly adorable. She vowed to make him do so again as soon as possible. Without thinking, she put the carrot she was holding into her mouth, only realizing as she bit down that it *was* a carrot.

She didn't like carrots.

Flavor burst into her mouth and Shelley chewed in wonder. "This is good," she admitted when she caught Tawny watching her.

"It's from my garden," Tawny said, pleased. "They're better than what you get at the store."

"I didn't think I liked carrots," Shelley said, still surprised by the delicious crunch.

"Maybe you just didn't have the right carrots," Tawny suggested.

There was a pounding on the steps as two boys making far more noise than their size indicated stomped up to the porch.

"Can we eat now?" Aaron asked, eyeing the table... particularly the end of the table with the cookies and pie.

"I'm *so* hungry," Trevor agreed. "Can we start with dessert?"

"Did you find all the eggs?" Shaun asked. "No food

until you've found them all."

They held up their battered baskets, which both appeared to have been involved in some kind of duel or possibly had been run over in the road. "We found nine of them."

"Eight," Aaron corrected.

"No, I have five," Trevor argued. "You have four. That's nine."

As they counted them over, Shelley asked Shaun in an aside, "What happens if they don't find them all?"

"We hope we don't find them with the lawnmower in a few weeks after they've ripened in the sun," Shaun replied with a knowing wince.

"That's probably enough eggs to earn some lunch," Tawny said peacefully, and no one waited for further invitation.

Settling into one of the Shaun's lawn chairs with a plate of food in the spring sunshine, Shelley thought that her whole life was like Tawny's carrots—something she'd thought she'd never like, and now something that she gleefully loaded onto her plate.

Aaron took a seat next to her, nearly upsetting his plate onto the lawn as he wiggled into his chair. "I like my new costume," he said around a mouthful of ham. "You're the best second mom ever!"

"That beats being second best," Shelley teased him. And, because she was a responsible adult, she added, "You're not supposed to talk with your mouth full." But she did it with her own mouth full, and winked at him.

"Oops," Aaron said, grinning so widely that a piece of ham fell out onto his lap.

"Your family puts out a great spread," Dean said, settling into the lawnchair on her other side while Shelley and Aaron giggled about his runaway ham.

Shelley's lion purred in contentment. This was, in every way, exactly where she belonged.

She had her mate, she had her *family*.

It didn't matter that her life wasn't the way she had planned, or that everything wasn't in neat, tidy boxes.

Kids were messy, and that was fine.

Life was messy, and that was fine, too.

They hadn't decided what to do when Dean had exhausted the parts of school that worked long-distance, and for some reason, it didn't bother Shelley not to have a plan. He might put the rest of the degree off until Aaron was out of elementary school. The hardware store was open again, but Dean hadn't reopened the shop.

She was a mess, sometimes, if less than before, and even that was fine.

She knew that whatever happened, wherever home ended up being, she'd found the people—and the dog—she would be there with.

"You good?" Dean asked with a sideways look.

Shelley smiled at him. "So good," she said sincerely. She leaned sideways in her lawn chair and Dean scooted to meet her with a kiss.

"Ewwww," said Aaron on her other side, but when Shelley sat back down into her chair, he impulsively put his plate down and threw his arms around her. She folded her arms around him and pressed her cheek to his.

"Am I good?" he asked cheerfully.

"So good," Shelley repeated.

Bingo, hearing the word *good*, came nosing into the action, all wiggling tail and hopeful ears.

"You're good, too," Shelley assured him.

And as far as he was concerned, that was all that mattered.

NOTE FROM ZOE CHANT

I hope you enjoyed Shelley and Dean's story! Green Valley is such a fun place to visit, and I'm already thinking about the next stories I'll tell here. Do you have a favorite character you'd like to see find a mate?

I always appreciate knowing what you thought – you can leave a review at Amazon or Goodreads or Bookbub (I read them all, and they help other readers find me, too!) or email me at zoechantebooks@gmail.com.

If you'd like to be emailed when I release my next book, please visit my webpage at zoechant.com to be added to my mailing list. You can also follow me on Facebook. You are also invited to join my VIP Readers Group on Facebook, where I show off new covers first, and you can get sneak previews, chances at free books, and I'll answer questions you might have.

The cover of *Bearly Together* was designed by Ellen Million – visit her page at ellenmillion.com to find coloring pages of some of my characters, including Gizelle (from Shifting Sands), Hugh (from Fire and Rescue), and more!

Fae Shifter Knights

Writing as Zoe Chant

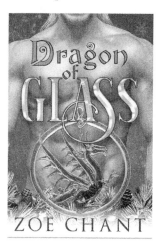

Book 1: **Dragon of Glass**

Jingle bells and magic spells!

Daniella has everything she needs for a quiet Christmas at home with her dog, Fabio. She's got way too much food, a real Christmas tree, a cable station streaming non-stop holiday movies, and even fruitcake. All she needs now is an ornament for her tree…

But what she gets instead is a glass dragon imprisoning a gorgeous naked guy from another world.

Trey, fae dragon knight, protector of the realm, and defender of the fallen crown, has finally been released from his spell by a kiss from a beautiful woman (and her noble hound). His power hobbled, his dragon form embarrassingly small, he finds himself navigating a strange world of wonders like televisions, refrigerators, and ham sandwiches, absolutely enspelled by a woman who swears she isn't a witch.

Then Trey discovers that the enemy from his homeworld is starting to spill into Daniella's and it will take power he no longer has to protect her... power that is locked in Daniella's heart.

THE DRAGON PRINCE OF ALASKA

Writing as Elva Birch

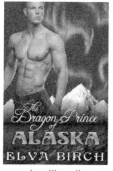

An unplanned promotion to princess!

Carina was just trying to advance to manager at her accounting firm. Instead, she uncovered the dirty secrets of a giant bank, got framed for murder, and fled the country. Now she's hiding out in a van with a stray dog in the kingdom of Alaska…

…And a gorgeous park ranger is telling her that she's his destiny (and also, camping illegally on royal land).

Before she knows it, she's whisked off to a palace on the arm of a dragon shifter (!) prince and fitted for a crown...because she's been chosen by an ancient magic spell to be the mate of the next king of Alaska.

As the youngest (and arguably most unsuitable) prince, Toren never thought that he would be tapped to rule, but he knows that Carina is worth the weight of his new duties. Now he's just got to figure out how to be a king, and even more importantly, how to protect his queen-to-be from old enemies...and new foes who will stop at nothing to see Alaska fall.

From the creator of the addictive and off-beat Shifting Sands Resort series comes a fresh new world of secret shifters and hidden magic. Set in an alternate world Alaska, where being a princess is more hiking boots and field hockey than it is tiaras and balls, THE DRAGON PRINCE OF ALASKA is a steamy, standalone, fast-paced paranormal romance adventure.

PROMPTED

Writing as Elva Birch

Prompted by readers, these twelve lyrical tales of magic and romance range from one hundred to one thousand words apiece, and from sweet to sizzling. They are elegantly crafted, bite-sized romantic romps, varying from humorous to heartbreaking. Shifters, fae, witches, and mortals find happiness and hope in unexpected places and forms.

PROMPTED is a sweet, satisfying quick read, not always straight, but always straight-up fun.

RAILS
Writing as Elva Birch

Bai knows better than to dream about his gorgeous Head of Files, Ressa. Fraternization at the Licensing Office is strictly forbidden, by his own ironclad decree. He should be content with their close friendship, and has almost convinced himself that he is.

Ressa knows there's something missing in her life. Her work, which has always been enough, leaves her feeling unsatisfied…even her secondary job with the prestigious Carnal Guild. She takes a lover, but swiftly realizes that what she thought were choices were clever orchestrations. Someone is playing her, and License Master Bai, in some larger, unknown plot.

Lives quickly unraveling, the only people that Bai and Ressa can trust are each other, and the bond of their friendship is sorely tested by secrets, betrayal, and the attraction for each other that they don't want to admit.

RAILS is a dark, tangled story full of murder, sex, unrequited love, drugs, prostitution, blackmail, and betrayal. There are no fairy tale happy endings…but there is hope that love can prevail.

Set in the shared world of Torn World, RAILS was released at tornworld.net in installments between 2010 and 2014. It has flavors of steampunk, fantasy, and light science fiction, moving between the glamorous high society of the Empire to the gritty criminal underworld.

SHIFTING SANDS RESORT

Writing as Zoe Chant

* Hot, strong, protective shifter heroes...who aren't jerks.
* Capable, complicated shifter heroines...who aren't doormats.
* Fresh new plots, not recycled stories, with unique magic and fantasy worldbuilding.
* ALL THE FEELS.
* Diverse leads: queer, disabled, multicultural, not all the same shape, the same color, or the same animal.
* A gorgeous tropical setting that you'll desperately wish you could visit.
* A complete 10 book series with a thrilling conclusion.

A luxury shifters-only resort on an island full of secrets...Shifting Sands Resort is the series you didn't know you were waiting for. Hot, hilarious, and heartwarming, each book is an electrifying standalone with a satisfying happy ever after...but they all tie together into an epic magical mystery that will leave you flying through the books.

Start the series with TROPICAL TIGER SPY, in which Tony Lukin uncovers the first of many mysteries and finds the love of his life.